He looked

It was like a blow ▓▓▓▓▓▓▓▓▓▓▓▓▓▓ her
breath away. Long ▓▓▓▓▓▓▓▓▓▓▓▓▓▓
face remained in her mind as clearly as if she still gazed
at it. Had she forgotten how beautiful he was? Had
she forgotten how much she loved him?

If she had, she remembered it now, and it brought the
emotion back in a flooding torrent.

Dear Reader

We have pleasure in introducing new author Rebecca Lang with MIDNIGHT SUN, set in Arctic Canada. Margaret Barker is back with THE DOCTOR'S DAUGHTER, then Judith Ansell and Marion Lennox take us to Australia, with HEARTS OUT OF TIME and ONE CARING HEART, both tear-jerkers! Enjoy your holiday reading.

The Editor

!!!STOP PRESS!!! If you enjoy reading these medical books, have you ever thought of writing one? We are always looking for new writers for LOVE ON CALL, and want to hear from you. Send for the guidelines, and start writing!

Judith Ansell is a doctor who has always had an interest in writing. She has worked in many different and sometimes exciting areas of medicine, and thus has an excellent background for writing Medical Romances. At present she combines part-time medical practice with writing for Mills & Boon and caring for her unruly two-year-old. She is married to a surgeon, and can affirm that doctors make excellent and patient husbands.

Recent titles by the same author:

THE CONSTANT HEART
A SPECIAL CHALLENGE
THE HEART'S HOME

HEARTS OUT OF TIME

BY
JUDITH ANSELL

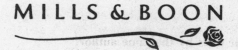

MILLS & BOON LIMITED
ETON HOUSE, 18-24 PARADISE ROAD
RICHMOND, SURREY TW9 1SR

*MILLS & BOON, the Rose Device and LOVE ON CALL
are trademarks of the publisher.*

*First published in Great Britain 1994
by Mills & Boon Limited*

© Judith Ansell 1994

*Australian copyright 1994   Philippine copyright 1994
This edition 1994*

ISBN 0 263 78705 2

Set in Times 10 on 11 pt.

03-9407-47069

Made and printed in Great Britain

CHAPTER ONE

EMMA TRELOAR, R.N., sank on to the seat in the sunny back garden of the new community clinic with shaking knees. Known for her calm efficiency as much as her dry sense of humour, Sister Treloar was anything but calm now. The news she had just received with outward serenity had whipped up an inner turmoil that made her heart race and her face burn.

Patrick Cavanagh! To work here in the new clinic that Emma had helped to set up! Dr Cavanagh, to whom she had been engaged over a year ago, and whose handsome face she had last seen racked with grief and anger as she had broken it off.

Emma sat in the sunshine of a crisp late winter Sydney day, and endeavoured to bring her emotions under control. She had seen Patrick's face so often before her in the past fourteen months, not only as it had been on that final, terrible day, but also as she had seen it in the beginning.

Emma had known at once that Dr Cavanagh was different. A tall, dark-haired Englishman whose readily tanning skin must, she concluded, have owed something to the Roman invasion, Patrick Cavanagh was a physician who had come to specialise in casualty work. Emma, two years qualified, had been working in Cas at Royal Prince Albert Hospital when he had been appointed director, and at once she had liked and respected him. He was brilliantly competent—a wonderful person to have in charge when the mangled victims of accidents were brought in, the ambulance

sirens blaring. But he was more than that. He cared
as much for the downtrodden folk who waited
miserably hour after hour in the dismal waiting-room
for someone to attend to their less dramatic ills. With
them he was gentle, patient, caring. Never dismissive,
as some of the other doctors were, he listened carefully
and made them feel they mattered. As one old lady
had said as she left, it made the wait worthwhile.
Emma saw that it worried him that they waited. This
was no bedside manner. The man really cared.

He was, of course, from the first moment when he
strolled into Casualty, swept his clear hazel eyes over
them and smiled, the pin-up of every nurse who was
inclined to be romantic. Something over six feet, with
an athletic frame and a strong handsome face, Patrick
Cavanagh could have had his choice of the nurses. It
had amazed Emma Treloar when first she had enter-
tained the idea, prompted by what her colleagues said
rather than any realisation of her own, that it was she
he especially liked.

She had put it down to the fact that they worked
well together, and admonished her colleagues not to
be silly. Emma Treloar was the 'best sort of nurse',
Sister Barker, in charge of Casualty, had been fond of
saying. She was quick and deft at her work, always
where she was wanted, and she kept her head in a
crisis. The patients saw her in a different way, but they
too approved. Young Sister Treloar was the one who
would always remember you, who would ask after little
Tommy's arm. She was cheerful and kind, and would
often make you laugh. She was good to look at, too.

Emma herself would have agreed with some of this,
but not with the latter. She would have said matter-of-
factly that her looks were very ordinary and it was a
good job she was useful. And it was true that Emma

lacked the sort of striking beauty that instantly drew all eyes. It was usually two days before the new resident realised that Sister Treloar was a very pretty girl. She had a sweet face, with large grey eyes that could be either grave or laughing. She wore her light brown hair neatly in a roll. Her mouth was the most delightful thing—it was small and well-shaped, calmly composed at one moment, then at the next turned up in an impish grin. About then it would also occur to the resident that there was something very nice about the way Emma Treloar looked in her nurse's uniform. She was of average height and slim, with a small waist accentuated by her uniform belt. But there was nothing wrong at all with the curves that appeared above or below it. These ruminations would often be followed by an invitation to dinner, but Emma steered clear of romantic involvement. She had not yet met the man who could interest her.

That was until Dr Cavanagh had come on the scene. Then it had quickly occurred to her that he interested her very much indeed. Emma had admonished herself to be sensible. He was thirty-two, some nine years older than her twenty-three, and she'd seen that he could take his pick. But Patrick Cavanagh had seemed to be a man who knew what he wanted. Quietly, with those clear hazel eyes and the warmth of his smile, he had wooed her, and in a few short weeks she'd found herself discovering feelings she had never known in his arms.

It had been like a wonderful dream. Clasped to his breast, with his lips on hers, she had known with a certainty that couldn't be shaken that he loved her. Composed and somewhat quiet with those around him, Emma alone had learnt of the intensity of passion that burnt within, and of the fierceness of her own answering feelings. After a few months, he'd asked her to marry him, and she'd known no doubt. She could only marvel at her unbelievable luck, till the events had occurred which altered everything.

Emma had schooled herself to her normal composure to talk to Evan Thomas, the co-ordinator of Community Health Services.

'Dr Cavanagh and Dr Fiona Whitely will be here on Monday,' said Evan. 'We'll have Monday for orientation and open the doors on Tuesday.' The bluff, cheerful doctor smiled at Emma. 'You've done a great job planning and setting up, Emma.' His eyes twinkled. 'We've managed to find doctors worthy of you, I think. Patrick's worked here before, in Cas at RPA. He's British. Saw our ad in the *Australian Medical Journal*. He's only arriving back from Britain tomorrow. By all accounts, he's very good indeed.'

Showing the presence of mind in an emergency which Sister Barker had valued, Emma mastered her mind, heart and voice and nodded. 'He is,' she said with remarkable calmness. 'I worked with him.'

'Did you, indeed?' he exclaimed. 'Well, that's nice. You'll be old friends.' Evan Thomas had clearly not heard of Emma's ill-fated engagement. She glanced at the faces of the other employees of the new clinic, and decided that none of them was aware of it either. Sister Helen Peters was a round-faced, cheerful girl of around Emma's age, who could be depended on to laugh at the dry jokes Emma was wont to make. She had come from another hospital to work in this clinic and knew nothing of Emma's history. Marje Gilbert and Anne Luck, the two receptionists, had worked at Royal Prince Albert, but in another department, and there was nothing in their faces to make Emma fear that they knew. She wondered for a moment whether she should tell them when Evan Thomas was gone, but quickly decided against it. Things would be awkward enough as it was without that. It was old gossip now. They'd probably never hear of it.

'Bye, Emma. See you Monday, love,' called Marje as Emma left the clinic. Emma waved her goodbye, and trod down the front path, her eyes sweeping over the sprawling complex of Royal Prince Albert Hospital, just across the road from them, where Emma had trained and worked till now. She paused when she reached the street, turning her back on the hospital gratefully, surveying the renovated Victorian house that was now the community clinic—a clinic which would serve the poor of the area. Its sign hung already on the green-painted cast-iron railing fence, promising free treatment and advertising their hours. Beyond the fence lay a small garden with wrought-iron seats in the shade of two pepper trees. Flowerbeds had been planted, ready to burst into bloom when spring arrived. The house itself looked pretty and welcoming.

Emma was sure she'd enjoy working here. It wasn't that she had disliked the hospital. It was a good hospital and she had learned all she knew there. But it was a busy place and it always seemed to have insufficient time and sympathy for the poor people who turned up with minor, or even sometimes major complaints at Casualty because they couldn't afford to go to a private doctor. Emma had felt especially sorry for them as they waited for hours in the corridor, ignored by the hard-pressed hospital staff. This clinic was a response to that problem. The hospital administration saw that it would take the load off the casualty staff. Emma hoped that it would offer the working-class people of the inner city the care they deserved.

As she walked to the bus stop through the gathering twilight, Emma's mind once more turned to Patrick Cavanagh. She could see why he'd applied to work at this clinic. He, too, had wished that more could be done for those people. But he couldn't have known when he accepted the post that Emma would be working at the clinic. Recalling their last meeting with painful clarity, Emma couldn't believe that he would have chosen to come here if that piece of information had been available. Against her will the memory assailed her. As she waited for her bus in the dim glow of the street-lamp, she lived again that other dreadful evening when she had known she must end their engagement.

He'd been a few minutes late that night, knocking briefly and letting himself in as he'd come to do. Swiftly he'd covered the sitting-room and given her a kiss and a smile that tore at her heart before he'd noticed that anything was wrong. Then her unresponsiveness or perhaps her pallor had drawn him up, and he'd said, 'Emma, is something the matter?'

She'd turned away from him, gripping the mantel shelf with two slim white hands, unable to look at his face as she'd told Patrick Cavanagh that she couldn't marry him after all.

There'd been no answer from him at first, and she'd been forced to turn and look at him. He'd stood there, a waiting look on his face, as though he was expecting her next words to confirm that this was one of Emma's jokes at which in a moment they'd be laughing together.

She had said no more, however, and the look had faded, to be replaced by another of horrified incomprehension. At the end of what seemed an eternity he'd spoken, his voice little more than a whisper. 'You mean it,' he said.

Emma nodded, the tears spilling out of her eyes and preventing speech. And then she saw that other look on his face, the one that would haunt her forever. It was one of rawest, most terrible pain. 'Why?' he breathed.

This was the hardest part. Emma knew she couldn't say it with his eyes on hers, so once again she turned away. She told him haltingly, her throat aching, her heart wrung. She had made a mistake. She didn't love him. Couldn't marry him. She was sorry.

Patrick's voice throbbed with anguish. 'I don't believe you!' he cried. He took her by the shoulders and tried to make her look at him. 'Emma! What is it? What's happened? Are you in some trouble?'

She kept her face turned away and only repeated what she'd said. A long silence followed. Emma could almost feel the man's desperate efforts to understand, to find an explanation other than the one which his mind all but refused to accept—that she was telling the truth.

She heard him take a ragged breath. 'I don't believe you,' he said again, but now she could hear the agony in it as the seconds ticked on and she made no move to rescind her words. 'Why?' he asked in a tortured tone.

Emma knew she must answer him. She knew what she must say. It would make him hate her, but that was the only kindness she could do him, the only help she could offer. She turned and willed herself to meet his gaze. 'Someone else,' she said.

The words hung between them. Patrick's eyes didn't shift from hers. He seemed frozen, his face under the tan as white as a sheet. Only his chest rose and fell too rapidly to show the effect of her words. 'How long?' he asked finally, his voice hoarse.

'From the beginning,' she steeled herself to say, her voice only collapsing at the end into a sob.

He flinched as though before a blow. He said not a syllable more. Only his face spoke for him in a language that seared Emma's heart. There his suffering was etched for her—the shock, the piercing grief, and finally the anger. Patrick stood silently and took one long last look at her. Then he turned on his heel and abruptly left the house.

Emma alone knew why she had done it, and that she had lied to him. She alone knew there was no one else and never had been, that she loved him desperately even as she denied it, and that fourteen long months had been insufficient to diminish that love one iota.

Emma filled the teapot from the urn with unsteady hands, and wished for the fortieth time that it were over. Yet again she glanced at the clock on the wall of the staffroom. One minute to nine. She knew an impulse to run for it, to drop the tray with the teacups and disappear forever rather than face the man whom she loved but had rejected. She knew she couldn't do it. And in another moment the sound of footsteps and voices told her it was too late anyway.

'Here they are,' whispered Helen Peters, and the two girls heard introductions being performed between the doctors and receptionists. Evan Thomas's hearty laugh rang out, joined by that of a female. Emma had the feeling of wanting to halt time, to put this meeting off until she was ready for it. In the same moment, she knew she could never *be* ready for it. And all at once it was upon her.

Evan Thomas came first, the new doctors following

behind him. Emma stood motionless, her hands clasped before her. Her face felt wooden, and her tongue seemed glued to the roof of her mouth. She doubted that she could say anything. Her eyes alone were mobile and swept the group in front of her to rest for a few seconds on the face of Patrick Cavanagh.

It was like a blow to the solar plexus. It took her breath away. Long after she had looked away, it remained in her mind as clearly as if she still gazed at it. Had she forgotten how beautiful he was? Had she forgotten how much she loved him? If she had, she remembered it now, and it brought the emotion back in a flooding torrent. He looked exactly the same.

Evan Thomas was speaking, making the introductions. Somehow Emma nodded at the dark face of Fiona Whitely, and stammered, 'H-how do you do?' And then he was speaking to Patrick, saying,

'No doubt you remember Emma Treloar? Once seen, never forgotten. Ha, ha!' blundering along in his bluff, cheerful way till Emma could have murdered him. She glanced again at Patrick's face to see how he was bearing it, and suffered a little shock to see that there was no emotion in his face at all.

'Yes, I certainly remember,' he said, and his voice was like his face. There was no undercurrent of feeling there, no hidden well of meaning. His tone was blandly sociable—conventionally polite. And suddenly Emma felt impelled to look at his eyes. They were the same as they always had been, and yet were different—the same beautiful clear hazel, but without the warmth they had always contained. Nor did there seem to be resentment. They told her nothing, though they met her own steadily. They were cool, bland, perhaps guarded, or perhaps just indifferent. He looked as

though the sight of Emma Treloar had not occasioned
a flutter in his pulse.

The dismay Emma felt told her clearly what her
hopes had been. She had hoped that he still cared for
her, that she could explain what she had done and beg
his forgiveness. She had half expected anger, and even
contempt, but she had hoped that he would listen to
her explanation and love her again as he had before.

Evan Thomas stayed long enough to have a cup of tea
with them. Emma was glad of his presence. While
Evan was there, there was no need to volunteer much
in the way of speech. He rattled on in his usual style
as the six staff members of the clinic sat round the big
table, Marje acting as mother as she inevitably would
and pouring the tea.

Emma, to divert her mind from Patrick, covertly
studied Fiona Whitely. She was pretty and outgoing,
with dark curling hair, dark eyes and a plummy
Melbourne accent. Emma wondered what the patients
would make of her and what sort of doctor she'd be.
She guessed she was part of the Melbourne social set,
and that Daddy would prove to be a prominent
Melbourne specialist. She thought suddenly that she
was judging too hastily. Or perhaps it was just that
she was completely thrown off balance to be sitting
across the table from Patrick Cavanagh.

Twice only did Emma's eyes stray back to him, and
each time she wished they hadn't. He had said very
little. That was not surprising. He had always been a
quiet man. But two years ago there had been a warmth
about him that made him approachable despite it. He
had preferred to listen, but his wonderful mouth would
often be curved in a smile, and his eyes would be
friendly.

His mouth was still strong and beautiful, but it didn't smile today, and his fine eyes held a look of cool remoteness. In other respects, Emma had been right in her first appraisal. There was little change. He looked as fit as ever. There were perhaps a few more grey hairs at his temples, but still only a light peppering among the dark. Perhaps the fine lines at the corner of his eyes were more marked, or perhaps it was just tiredness from his long flight.

'Well, I'll get out of your way,' said Evan Thomas, 'and then you girls can show Fiona and Patrick around.'

'Would you like another cup?' Marje said to Patrick. 'There's plenty in the pot.' It was inevitable that Marje would try to mother him. 'You must be tired, coming all that way,' she added, starting stright away.

For the first time, Emma saw Patrick Cavanagh respond a little. His lips curved, just enough to remind Emma's heart of what a smile from Patrick Cavanagh was like. 'No, thank you, Marje. You're very kind,' he said. He still has nice manners, Emma thought, recovering from the sensations which had invaded her. But she noticed that the smile he'd given Marje had failed to reach his eyes.

'He's a bit of a cool fish,' remarked Anne in a low voice as she took out her sandwiches. She needn't have worried about being overheard. The doctors had gone to the administration building to fill out the inevitable forms that came with starting a new job.

Helen answered, 'Yeah. He's a bit—you know—intimidating.'

Marje settled her considerable weight in a chair. 'He'll be all right,' she said placidly. 'He's just done in. And he doesn't know us.'

'He knows Emma,' Helen objected. 'What's he like, Em?'

Emma controlled her voice admirably. 'He's a nice man,' she said. 'He cares about the patients. I think he'll be excellent.'

'He doesn't seem very friendly,' put in Anne.

'He's quiet,' Emma told them. 'He's quite friendly, really.' Even as she said it, though, she wondered whether she was telling them the truth about Patrick Cavanagh now. Had he changed? And had she done that to him? Was that impassive coldness the result of his experience with her? What else had happened to him in the past fourteen months when she hadn't even known where he was? They were questions without any answers. Emma could only try to eat her lunch, though she had very little appetite after the stresses of the morning.

CHAPTER TWO

EMMA's afternoon boded fair to be equally stressful. It would be spent in acquainting the doctors with every aspect of the clinic. They started in the front room of the converted house—the old sitting-room—which had been adapted to serve as the waiting-room. It was businesslike, with a long desk, filing cabinets and chairs, but it was still cosy, with the fine old fireplace still there and in working order. Emma had the secret ambition of getting it going in winter. Then the waiting-room would be a homelike place for the patients to come to.

She was happy to leave Anne and Marje to take charge of the doctors for a while. They explained the appointment system, and made them familiar with the records and the stationery.

But then it was the nurses' turn. Emma would have gladly left it to Helen, but Helen hung back, expecting Emma to take the lead. It was understandable. Emma had been in on the planning and equipping of the clinic. It was she who had stayed late many nights with John Morrison, the young medical administrator, poring over the plans and drawing up endless lists to make sure they had forgotten nothing. If there was anything inefficient about the place, anything essential missing, she must share the blame. But she didn't think there was.

So she took control of herself and slowly showed them through the the rest of the centre, acutely aware of Patrick Cavanagh's tall figure despite the fact that her eyes hardly touched him as he followed quietly in her wake. She took them carefully over the two consulting-rooms, the treatment-room where minor procedures could be done, and the stores-room where their stocks of medicine and materials were kept. It was very orderly, and Emma's exposition of it coherent and thorough. Fiona Whitely congratulated her several times. Patrick Cavanagh merely nodded briefly and said, 'Very good,' his hazel eyes barely grazing her own.

It gave her only a little satisfaction to see that he was no more outgoing with Fiona when she turned to him in the treatment-room, saying, 'I think I'm going to have to rely on your superior wisdom, Patrick. I haven't much experience in some of these procedures.'

Though her remark was accompanied by a little fluttering of the lashes and a winning smile, Patrick didn't look specially gratified. 'I'm happy to help,' he said in a polite but non-committal way. 'Is there cautery?' he asked Emma abruptly.

Emma nodded. 'Chemical and electrical,' she replied. 'The diathermy machine lives here.' She uncovered it where it lay on a wheeled table handy to the examination couch. A machine the size of a small typewriter supplied power to a knife which could either be used to cut or to seal off bleeding vessels. Patrick Cavanagh came to stand beside her, looking over her shoulder. Emma tried not to let it unnerve her. 'It plugs in here,' she explained. 'It's got quite a long lead, so you can wheel it up to the couch easily.'

He took the business end—the slim blade with its handle—from her hand, just brushing it with his own. Emma felt a current through her almost as though the machine had been switched on. If Patrick Cavanagh felt anything, he didn't betray it by as much as a blink.

He held the instrument in his hand a moment, then said, 'Nice,' in an impassive tone and handed it back with the briefest glance at her face.

Even that was enough to affect Emma. After fourteen months of longing for him, of wondering where he had gone after she had broken their engagement, to have him standing close beside her, to have touched his hand, was almost more than she could bear. Memories rushed in on her and almost overwhelmed her—of his smile and his voice as he told her he loved her, of his lips on hers, and the way it had felt to be held in those arms.

There was no sign that Patrick Cavanagh was similarly affected. He asked a few more questions in the same impersonal way and volunteered no remarks unconnected with what they were examining. His face, when she dared to glance at it, was as handsomely composed as before.

Towards the end of their tour, Emma began to have a sense of unreality. This couldn't be happening. For so long she had thought of this meeting—dreamed of it, longed for it. And now that they stood in the same room he was treating her as though she were a total stranger who had never meant anything to him at all. Was it the result of veiled hostility? Or had he simply recovered from his love for her, as she had not? At the thought of that, a great chasm of despair seemed to yawn at her feet.

'What do you think they'll want to do this afternoon?' asked Helen.

'I suppose talk to us about how they want to do things. What they want us to do,' Emma answered.

'Bags I work with Dr Fiona,' Helen said, and Emma felt a tension seize her.

'Why? I think you'd get on very well with Dr
Cavanagh,' she said quickly, but Helen shook her head
emphatically.

'No way. The strong, silent type makes me nervous.
And you know how useless I am when I'm
nervous, Emma.'

Emma tried to laugh. 'Don't be silly,' she said, and
added haltingly, 'He might—prefer you.'

'He'd have to be daft,' averred her friend. 'You're
the best nurse anywhere. Anyway, you know him
already. He's yours.'

Emma had been right. When the doctors returned after
lunch, Fiona sat down at the table and Patrick, leaning
his tall frame against the bench, said, 'I suppose we'd
better discuss how we're to organise things.'

It wouldn't be very much different from working
in Casualty. The nurses would carry out preparatory
observations when necessary, would ready patients for
procedures, carry out the doctors' orders, have their
own routine work as varied as doing daily dressings
and weighing babies. Unless he'd changed in this
respect too, Emma already had a fair idea of how he
liked things done.

'I guess it's sensible if one of you works with one
of us,' observed Fiona, and Helen lost no time in leap-
ing into the opening.

'Yes, we thought that,' she said. 'And since Emma
has already worked with Dr Cavanagh, we thought she
could work with him and I could work with you.'

Emma felt herself blushing to the roots of her hair.
'We' hadn't thought any such thing, but Helen had
beaten her to it, and there was nothing she could do. In
agony, she waited for Patrick Cavanagh to comment.

'Does that suit you, Patrick?' Fiona asked.

There was a brief but definite pause before he said tonelessly, 'Of course.'

For some reason that tiny tell-tale hesitation made Emma feel better rather than worse. From it she concluded that he would have preferred not to work with her. Had he been able to think of a way of escaping it, he would have done so. That might hurt, but at least it made her feel more in touch with reality. From his behaviour up till now, the events of fourteen months ago might almost not have happened. He had seemed perfectly untouched by any emotion at seeing her again. That one split-second's pause had suggested it wasn't so. He *was* still human, after all. There *was* some feeling behind the mask, even if it was only anger and dislike.

'All right. In that case, Helen,' said Fiona, rising to her feet, 'why don't we go and look at the dressings we have? I'll show you which ones I prefer to use for what.'

As Helen Peters followed Fiona to the door, a tide of panic swept through Emma. Patrick still lounged against the staffroom bench. The receptionists were busying themselves out in the waiting-room. In a few seconds, Emma and Patrick were alone.

It was too soon for Emma. She hadn't had time to gather her thoughts. She wanted to see him alone, of course. She wanted to tell him what had happened, to explain. But she needed time to think about it first, to work out how to say it, to think what the reaction of this new Patrick might be.

She sat in silence, her heart pounding in her chest. After an uncomfortable span of time, she willed herself to look in his direction. His eyes, calm and passionless, were on her face. It made her heart plunge, but she didn't look away. This had to come. They must say something to one another. She groped in her mind for a way to start.

Patrick forestalled her. 'I don't have to tell you how I like things done,' he remarked quietly. 'You already know.'

There was silence again. Was that all he was going to say? Emma herself nodded dumbly.

And then he went on. 'We worked well together once. There's no reason—on my side—that we can't do so again.'

Emma found her tongue. 'Patrick, I——' she began, but she saw him give a tiny shake of his head, and was stilled.

Not a vestige of emotion flickered in his eyes or his tone as he told her, 'Don't. There's nothing to say. I'm sorry—you weren't given more warning of my coming here. I realise you were only told on Friday.'

'D-did you know—I'd be here?' she managed to ask.

The man's hazel eyes dwelt on her coolly. 'No.' His tone was flat. It didn't speak dismay, but neither did it reveal any happiness in the fact. It was entirely even.

Emma gazed at him for a long moment, trying to marshal her thoughts. How could she begin to say what she wanted to in the face of this? He didn't want to hear.

'You've put a great deal of work into this place,' he observed. 'I'm aware that you probably regret my presence. But I shan't make things difficult for you.'

Emma desperately wanted to utter a disclaimer—to tell him that the strongest of all the emotions she had felt when told about it were hope and joy, and that these had quickly outstripped the dismay and the fear. It seemed an impossible thing to say to this Patrick. The stern, unsmiling face before her robbed her of her courage, for all that it was just as beautiful as before.

Emma loved him too much to bear a rebuff. She knew it would tear her apart. Even uncertainty was better than that.

'Are you—are you well?' she asked, not knowing what else to say.

There was a pause during which his face maintained its severity, then for the second time that day his mouth softened just a fraction. 'Don't I look well?' he enquired with a hint of dryness.

'Y-yes. You do.' In her mind, Emma added glumly, You look wonderful. You look what you always were—the most devastatingly handsome man I've ever met.

'Are *you* well?' Was it an ironic question, or was it sincere?

'Yes, perfectly,' Emma answered briefly, and with that they seemed to run out of conversation altogether. She cursed herself for her inanity, and knew she had to escape this impossible situation, at least for now. 'I hope—you like it here,' she stammered, with which further inanity she came to her feet, excused herself and ducked away.

In the event, the community clinic treated its first patient that very day. Emma reached the waiting-room in time to see Marje Gilbert bearing a howling toddler up the path, followed by a rather grubby urchin of about eight years old.

'I think we've got a job for you here, Sister Emma,' she said. 'I saw this tot crying on the footpath. They were playing there. This is her brother, Mark. He'll tell you what the trouble is.'

'She put play dough up 'er nose,' Mark announced. 'She's ony three,' he added, in exculpation of the crime.

Marje Gilbert shook, and Emma struggled to keep
her countenance. She was unable to stop her mouth
from turning up a little at the corners, but she spoke
with creditable calm. 'Oh, well. That's not as awkward
as a plastic Teenage Mutant Ninja Turtle. And I've
managed to fish one of those out in my time.'

''Ave you?' Mark asked. It seemed to raise Emma
in his esteem.

'Yes. And very difficult it was, too. They're a tricky
shape. What's your sister's name?'

It was Kylie.

Emma took her from Marje's arms. 'Don't cry,
Kylie. We'll get the play dough out again. What colour
was it?' she enquired conversationally. She moved
towards the treatment-room as she spoke, motioning
for Mark to come along, too.

Kylie stopped crying, evidently arrested by the difficult task of deciding what colour it was. Emma sat her
on the couch, and noticed that Patrick Cavanagh had
come curiously to the door. 'Do you know what colour
it was, Kylie?' Emma continued, intent on distraction.

Kylie didn't, but she solved the problem by holding
out to Emma the lump she carried in her pocket.

'Oh! Blue!' said Emma. She darted a glance in the
direction of Patrick as she asked, 'Is the play dough
in your nose the same colour as that?' Out of the
corner of her eye, Emma saw Patrick's mouth quirk
as he got the message.

'I know. We'll have a look.' Kylie saw no reason to
protest as Emma shone a pencil torch up one little
nostril. 'A-a-ah!' she exclaimed. 'Yes, it is. A pretty
blue.' Emma reached for a packet of tissues, and in
response to the doctor's querying eyebrow murmured,
'Quite a long way.'

Kylie strove hard to blow her nose for Emma, but

it was not an operation she'd really mastered. At the end of ten minutes, they were forced to admit defeat.

'What are you gonna do now?' asked Mark with interest.

'Dr Patrick is going to have a look now,' Emma said, anticipating the next move. She handed him the headlamp. Patrick positioned himself on a stool in front of his little patient, and introduced himself gravely. Kylie had no objection to his looking with the light of the headlamp, but Emma knew it would be a different story when the Tilley's forceps appeared. She hoisted herself on to the couch beside the child and hugged her to her side.

'Do you know, Dr Patrick's come all the way from England in an aeroplane?' she announced.

'Why?' asked Kylie. Emma privately thought it was a very good question. 'To take the play dough out of little girls' noses,' she answered, and was rewarded to see a spasm cross the doctor's previously immobile face. 'Will you be a good girl and be very still? What do you think that is, up there on the wall?'

'Nice try,' commented Dr Cavanagh drily a few minutes later when it became clear that the task wasn't going to be accomplished so easily. Kylie didn't feel that Tilley's forceps were things she wished to have up her nose. She infinitely preferred play dough, and lost no time in making her preference loudly known.

'Will you take her a moment, please, Doctor?' Emma asked, and Patrick complied, to be immediately beaten about the head by two diminutive but angry fists.

Emma struggled not to smile as she positioned herself on the couch, knees apart, to receive the child back.

'I've noted that grin, Sister,' Patrick murmured, and

it forced a little choke of laughter from her. He thrust the tiny termagant back into Emma's lap. Emma clamped Kylie between her knees, holding her body with one arm and her head with the other hand. Ignoring all words of reassurance, Kylie struggled for all she was worth.

Emma gasped. 'I hope you're going to be quick, Doctor.'

'I thought I'd pop out for a cup of tea,' he said blandly, drawing from her another involuntary spurt of laughter. Well, at least he still had a sense of humour, she thought gratefully. Then in another moment he had reached carefully up with the Tilley's forceps, and drawn the foreign body out.

Kylie stopped crying immediately, and Emma breathed a sigh of relief. The child demanded to see what he'd recovered, and when he showed her held out her ball of dough for him to place what he'd fished out with the rest.

'Oh! Kylie—I don't think we should put the play dough that's been in your nose with the rest, do you?' asked Emma.

Her eyes flashed up to Patrick's to see whether he was amused. His face was almost entirely composed as he said, 'Waste not, want not, Sister.'

For the first time, her laugh was unrestrained. She thought she saw a relaxation of his features, too, but then his eyes flicked down and Emma realised at once that her skirt, in the struggle, had ridden halfway up her thighs. Emma blushed. 'Would you mind taking her, please, Doctor?' she asked in a strained tone.

Her pulse speeded up as Patrick Cavanagh's eyes seemed to linger on the expanse of shapely leg. Silently he removed the child from her lap. But his eyes remained on her a moment longer as she hitched down her skirt.

Emma reached the quiet street where she lived in the dark. Another Victorian house, much smaller than that which housed the clinic, awaited her, along with a tough-looking ginger cat who signalled his impatience with his moth-eaten tail.

'Hold your horses,' commanded Emma sternly, and he answered with a rusty 'miaow'. Tiger, as she called him, had come with the house. After a few uncertain days, they had decided to tolerate one another. Tiger accepted her as the source of catfood, and Emma accepted him as a sporadically efficient pest exterminator. Any suggestion that they also put up with one another out of loneliness would have been crossly denied by them both.

Emma fed him and retired to an armchair with a drink. She was profoundly fatigued. But she didn't feel as hopeless as she had earlier that day. Just that flicker of humour in Patrick Cavanagh had made her feel better. Perhaps there was hope, if she could summon the courage to tell him why she had broken off their engagement. Emma rubbed the scar on her thigh, as she always did unconsciously when she thought of that time.

As happy as it was possible to be, loved and in love, Emma had had no way of seeing what was coming two years ago. It had been the end of winter. Spring had beckoned, and so had the four-week holiday that she and Patrick were going to have together. She'd intended to take him home to the North Coast town where her parents lived. They would make plans there for their wedding.

She had found the lump on her very last day before

the holidays. It was only a small lump, towards the bottom of her femur—the bone in her thigh. It was only half an inch in diameter, but it was definitely there and slightly tender. She had known she mustn't ignore it.

She had worked with Dr Watts on Orthopaedic, and he'd laughingly said he was only too pleased to look at her leg. When he did, however, she'd seen him stop smiling, and she'd known the first tiny tremor of fear.

After that, it had all happened much too quickly. They had X-rayed it straight away, taking a wearying number of shots from different angles, and soon Emma was in an empty office in the radiology department, facing Leon Watts again, whose every feature Emma remembered as though it had been engraved on her brain.

Good, kind Leon had taken her hand, and she'd known from his face what he was going to say. 'Emma—I'd like to tell you this is nothing to worry about.' He had paused for a moment as though he didn't know how to go on. 'I can't. From the form of that lump on the X-ray, I have to say that there are nine chances out of ten that it's a tumour. An osteo-sarcoma.'

Emma's eyes hadn't wavered. She had kept them on his, even as the brutal reality of what he was saying had gouged its way into her mind.

'We need to do a biopsy. As soon as possible. Then we have to decide what to do.'

It was clear to Emma that the biopsy was a formality. Leon Watts was already sure. Nine chances out of ten, he had said, but that was only a formula, a way of breaking the news a little more gently. She had a can-cerous growth in the bone of her leg. It might be going to kill her. Her only hope would be to have an

amputation halfway up the thigh. There was no other
treatment for osteosarcoma, and delay could be fatal.

She had seen people take this sort of news, and she
knew she was doing just as most of them did. She
didn't cry. She felt numb, empty, the horror of it too
great to encompass, the enormity of it driving out
rational thought. She escaped when she could, walking
woodenly, automatically returning to Casualty for her
bag and bidding people goodnight. Patrick was at a
meeting. She wouldn't see him till nine oclock, when
he'd call by her house.

It was only then, with that thought, that her brain
seemed to grind agonisingly into action, and she
decided she would walk home across the park and
through the darkening streets, for now at last she'd
begun to cry.

Patrick. How to tell Patrick? And she knew almost at
once that she wouldn't. It was impossible. She couldn't
marry him now.

She thought of all the plans they had made, the
things they intended to do. They wanted to work in
the Outback. They planned to go next year—to join
the Aboriginal Health Service for a few years, perhaps
do a stint with the Flying Doctors. Plenty of time
to do everything before they had a family.

Emma choked on a rending sob. By this time next
week, she would have her leg amputated mid-thigh.
And be waiting for it to heal to see whether she would
ever be able to walk on an artificial one. There would
be no outback, no Flying Doctor Service. How could
she even think of having babies, with only one leg
and uncertain even then if she would live to see them
grow up?

Patrick didn't need a wife with one leg. Emma tried
to imagine making love to him, and couldn't bear it.

She couldn't tell him. He would want to marry her anyway. She knew his character. He would stick by her. But the rest of his life would be spent in regretting it, and in trying not to let her see it was so. She wouldn't do it to him, or to herself.

She knew what she had to do. And she couldn't even wait till after the biopsy. Then it would be too late, for he would have to know about it.

Somehow Emma found the resolution to break off their engagement, and to tell him the only lie she could think of that would convince him that she wanted it so. As director of Casualty, Patrick Cavanagh worked long hours and spent half his nights on call. He had no way of knowing that there'd never been anyone else at all.

Emma had attended Dr Watts' clinic for a biopsy the following day, oblivious to any pain beside the agony in her heart. She had told no one, preferring to face it alone. Leon Watts had been kind. The results would be ready quickly, the very next day. Would she like him to come and tell her at home? No. She would come to the hospital. It hardly seemed to matter. What was the loss of a leg?

And yet as she waited next day for the doctor her own sense of self-preservation came to the fore. She found her heart pounding as she sat in the waiting-room, and questions crowding her brain. How advanced was it? How aggressive? Would amputation save her, or was it a waste of time? Had it already spread?

With her mind busy with such themes, Emma simply failed at first to understand him. It was Leon Watts' face that finally got the message across rather than his words. For his face wore the broadest possible smile. And one word finally assumed meaning for her among all the others. The word was 'benign'.

Benign. Emma said it in a croaking voice. Benign.
Leon Watts' speech washed over her, half compre-
hended. 'Wouldn't have predicted it...one shot in
ten...delighted...small operation...take out the
lump...no need to worry.' Then, finally, she'd burst
into tears.

Anyone who thinks the world is not a beautiful place
needs only to be sentenced to death and then
reprieved, Emma thought as she walked across the
park in the sunshine. It was a moment of exhilarating
joy and relief.

It was only a mile to Patrick's house. In celebration
of the fact of having two legs both of which were going
to stay where they were, Emma decided to walk it.
Over and over as she strode along she saw his face—
saw him receive her, perhaps unwillingly at first, saw
him listen to her, saw his expression—horrified perhaps for a while, perhaps even angry, but in the end
relieved, happy, reconciled to her, their future together
once more secure. She imagined being held in his arms,
hearing her name spoken by him, his lips on her own.
For the last hundred yards, she ran, arriving at his
door flushed and breathless.

A stranger opened the door. Emma asked for
Patrick. Slowly, the man shook his head. Not here, he
was afraid. He looked Emma over thoughtfully. Look,
why didn't she come in?

Only a few moments sufficed for Emma to be in
possession of the facts. Patrick Cavanagh was gone.
She sat stunned in the chair that the man had offered
her and listened to what he had to say. Bradley was
his name, an acquaintance of Patrick's. He'd been
looking for a place to stay for some time. Then Patrick
had rung him suddenly the night before last to say he

was going away. He could stay here. Tim Bradley had
taken Patrick to the airport yesterday, seen his plane
take off. A sudden decision, but he'd had four weeks'
holiday coming and had used that in lieu of notice at
the hospital. He'd decided to work with Community
Aid Abroad. Bradley wasn't sure where—didn't think
Patrick knew yet. He was headed for London. He
supposed they'd post him from there.

Emma calmed herself. OK, it wasn't good, but it
wasn't the end of the world. Patrick could be contacted. It might take some time, but it could be
mended. She had a month's holiday to apply herself
to the task.

But, despite letters, telephone calls and telegrams,
at the end of a month it seemed that Patrick Cavanagh
had vanished into thin air. CAA hadn't heard of him.
The British Medical Board agreed that he was registered there, but there was no reply from the address
they had. He had a sister in Britain, but Emma didn't
know where she lived, or even her married name.
Every other idea she had came to nothing. Short of
calling out Interpol, there was no way of finding out
where he was unless he contacted Bradley. Emma
thought at first that he must. Bradley would pay the
household bills, but there must be other mail. As the
weeks and then the months went by, however, Emma
began to realise that Patrick must have written with a
change a address to anyone that mattered. For
Bradley, like her, heard nothing.

CHAPTER THREE

EMMA had given up gradually. For a long time she had continued to hope that something would be heard of Patrick. After a number of months she had contacted Community Aid Abroad again, in case he'd taken a holiday before he joined up, but the result was just the same as the last time. Bradley had taken over the lease of Patrick's house when it ran out, and hadn't heard from him either. There had been no stone left to turn, and nothing to try. Emma had had to accept that the gods had toyed with them cruelly, and that she would probably never see him again.

Emma Treloar was outwardly the same. She did her work, saw her parents and her friends, even after a time made the same wry jokes. Only Emma knew that she could never be the same again, that there was a place on the inside that would be forever empty. The wound where the cyst had been removed from her bone was healed, the scar small and faint. The scar inside her was ugly and jagged, and threatened to break open each time she saw someone who looked a little like him, or who bore his name, or even his nationality.

Emma sighed and finished her drink. If she told him what had happened, would he forgive her? He must have been so angry. He must believe her to be the worst kind of cheat. And even if he was no longer angry and contemptuous, could he still care about her?

* * *

'I didn't think we'd see any customers for days!' exclaimed Anne.

'Neither did Marje,' observed Emma drily. 'She went touting in the street for them yesterday.' The girls laughed. 'It's the notices in Cas,' Emma explained. 'People are coming from there. I think you'll find we're very busy within a week.'

It was true. An ordinary general practice setting up could expect business to be slow at first. But patients were being diverted here already from across the road. They came tentatively, looking uncertain as to their right to be here. But Marje and Anne soon made them welcome. And the sight of Sister Treloar heartened them, too. Here was someone they knew, and who knew them.

'Hello, Mr Billings,' she called. 'How's that grandson of yours who thinks he's an eagle? Sad case,' she said to Marje with mock-solemnity. 'Keeps climbing into trees and trying to fly away.'

Mr Billings cackled with delight. ''E's terrific now, thanks, Sister. 'Is 'ead an' 'is arm 'ave 'ealed.' The old man wheezed with laughter as he prepared to make a joke of his own. ''E eats like a vulture!' he said, and crowed joyfully when Emma gave a gurgle of good-natured laughter.

All day long they trooped across from Cas, and a few drifted in from the street as well, having seen the sign. Many of them Emma knew. Some she didn't. There weren't enough of them to make them busy, but there were enough to stop them being bored. They proceeded through the day at a leisurely pace that made a nice change from Casualty for both the staff and the patients.

Emma had come to work today resolved on being calm and composed. She had to work with Patrick, and whatever her feelings or his the work must be done efficiently. Till an opportunity came for Emma to make her confession, till Patrick Cavanagh showed her that he was interested in hearing it, she would treat him professionally. She would not let him affect her.

Even so, when she first saw him the feelings surged up in her anyway. He was sprawled in one of the staffroom chairs, his long legs stretched out in front of him, a morning cup of tea at his hand. For a moment he kept his eyes to the paper he was reading, and Emma was able to examine his face again in the light of morning. Yes, there were some tiny new lines beside his eyes, but they didn't detract from his attractiveness at all. It was a lean, tanned, strong face, the straight nose and defined jaw full of decision. The dark hair curled just a little over the broad forehead, and a matching set of dark eyebrows overhung the fine eyes. The mouth was strong, too, and beautifully shaped, with a sensual curve to the lower lip that suggested a passionate side to his nature normally hidden behind his quiet civility.

Emma hung her coat on the peg and laboured to suppress the muddle of emotions—pain, apprehension and longing. When she turned again, he looked up and accorded her a polite good morning.

'Good morning,' Emma answered, and poured herself a heart-starting cup of tea.

'Quite a cool morning,' he volunteered, and Emma agreed with him.

'I saw some wattle out, though,' she added.

'Ah! It won't be long till it's warm, then.'

Emma suddenly wondered if they were ever going to be able to utter more than polite inanities. She finished her tea, and, since he was silent again, left him to go and find some work to do.

Their morning conversation set the tone for the day.
When the first patients appeared they started work,
Emma bringing them to him and retiring till summoned
by the buzzer to help with something or to carry out
his orders. She positioned a young mother for a Pap
smear and stayed to assist, cut a plaster off an arm
and cleaned and dressed an elderly lady's leg ulcer.
Throughout it all, Patrick was courteous and considerate, but as cool and remote as he was once warm and
intimate. Emma couldn't help it—it smote her; and as
the day wore on the memories assailed her. It was the
very contrast with the past that produced them and
made them so clear. She remembered how they had
worked together in Casualty—the smiles, the jokes
made, the meeting of eyes when something had happened that they wanted to share. She recalled to her
mind Patrick's eyes dancing with laughter over the
head of a patient, or resting on her warmly for a
moment as she crossed the room. There was nothing
of that now. His gaze, if it coincided briefly with hers,
was impersonal. He didn't smile at her at all. She began
to feel she would prefer anger and resentment to this.
Could she ever bring herself to say what she must to
this self-contained, almost frosty man?

He had buzzed her. 'Sister, we need to remove
this little lump from Mrs Wilby's arm. As you can
see, it's a basal cell tumour. Will you take Mrs
Wilby to the treatment-room and get things ready,
please?'

Emma nodded. 'Yes, Doctor.' But Mrs Wilby, an
old lady who had never had a skin lesion removed,
had begun to dab at her eyes. Emma quickly put a
hand on her shoulder. 'Mrs Wilby,' she said softly,
'there's nothing whatever to worry about!'

'I'm sorry,' gulped the old lady. 'I feel so silly. You

must think I'm a foolish old woman. I'm so sorry, Doctor.'

Patrick slid forward in his chair and reached out for her hand, taking and covering it with his own two large ones. '*I'm* sorry,' he said. 'I don't know how I could be such a fool—rushing you like that.'

Mrs Wilby's eyes flew to his face. 'Oh, no, no!' she gasped.

Emma saw him give her hand a squeeze. 'Can you forgive me?' he asked.

Mrs Wilby was covered in pleasant confusion as the best-looking doctor in Sydney smiled down into her eyes. 'Oh, no—I mean—it wasn't—Doctor, you didn't!'

'I think I did,' he said with gentle regret. 'You've never had a bump taken off before, have you? The idea takes a little getting used to. I don't think you're silly at all.'

Mrs Wilby's eyes brimmed again with grateful tears. 'So—kind——' she murmured inarticulately.

'It's actually very easy,' he explained. 'And very quick. I won't hurt you at all.'

'Oh, no, I'm sure you won't!' she cried.

Emma led the elderly lady to the treatment-room. One question at least had been answered to her satisfaction. Patrick Cavanagh had not lost his ability to care about his patients. There at least his emotions were intact. It had been both a pleasure and a grief to see the cool façade roll back—a pleasure to see that he still did have feelings, a grief to think he might have none for her.

The minor operation was soon accomplished. Emma stood at Dr Cavanagh's side to help as he quickly excised the skin cancer with the deftness and expertise that Emma well remembered. She watched his hands

in the surgical rubber gloves as they swiftly cut an
ellipse of skin around the lesion with the gleaming
blade of the scalpel. They were quite large hands,
strong and beautifully shaped. Emma had often been
surprised that they could work so delicately and feel
so gentle. He lifted the excised skin away, and Emma
dabbed at the welling redness which appeared in its
place with a square of white gauze, handing him the
needle-holders with the suture in their jaws with the
other hand. She dabbed periodically as he sutured,
the only sound the rhythmic click-click of the needle-
holders as they opened and closed on the needle. Seven
perfectly spaced stitches drew the wound together,
each cut to the same length by Emma's scissors. They
worked with the same physical harmony they'd always
known together, their gloved hands moving in a surgical ballet of perfect action, anticipation and response.

Soon Mrs Wilby was being helped from the table
where she'd lain, a white stick-on dressing on her arm.

'It didn't hurt a bit!' she was saying.

Patrick smiled and squeezed her shoulder. 'That
bump will never trouble you again. Sister will take
your stitches out in a week. Sister Treloar is better at
taking stitches out than anyone in the southern hemisphere. She won't hurt you at all.'

'Only the southern hemisphere, Doctor?' asked
Sister Treloar in an offended voice.

Mrs Wilby laughed. Emma glanced at Patrick and
saw that he had smiled obediently. Emma had the
distinct impression, however, that it was a smile that
did not reach his eyes.

Only once was there a moment when he, too, might
be wrestling with memories. All nurses had their own
ways of doing things, their own idiosyncrasies. Emma
had one that had always made him laugh. When

patients had their ears syringed to remove the wax, the water had to be round about body temperature. Water too cold or hot would make the patient dizzy. There was sufficient leeway for most people simply to test the water with their hands, but Emma liked to measure it with a thermometer. Patrick had often teased her about it.

Mr McGarrity sat in the chair in the treatment-room with a towel around him, waiting for Dr Cavanagh to syringe his ears. Normally Emma would do it, but he had an ear infection, which made it a job for Patrick.

'I won't keep you long, Doctor,' she said, dipping a thermometer into the water jug. 'I like to measure the temperature.'

There was a pause for a moment, then she heard Patrick say in a dry tone, 'I recall.' And at last, when her eyes flicked up at him, she could see a tiny glimmer of something in his own. They fell away quickly before hers, but it had been enough to make Emma's heart speed up and a feeling of sweet tension gather in her. When she looked at him again, however, he was just as sombre and unapproachable as before.

Nor did his manner change when Fiona Whitely came to ask his opinion about a patient she was seeing. He listened attentively and gave his advice, but he didn't respond to her bright smile in any perceptible way. Emma found herself feeling glad. It was clear to her if it wasn't to him that Fiona was already interested in him. She had hung on his words, looking seductively up through her lashes in a way that Emma found nauseating. Emma began to think she didn't care for her much.

Then, with the last patient of the day, something of their old communication seemed to spring up. Patrick had brought her to the treatment-room.

'Sister, this is Ellen Fleet. Sister Emma Treloar, Ellen.'

Emma faced a worn-looking woman of perhaps thirty, with a defeated face. It was also a face disfigured by bruises and lacerations—none so deep as to require stitches, but needing Emma's services to clean them up.

'Ellen tells me she fell down the stairs,' Dr Cavanagh remarked in a bland voice. But Emma knew the tone, and her eyes flew to his face. Over the head of the patient he regarded her steadily. Only a certain grimness and something in the intentness of his gaze told Emma exactly what he thought.

'I see.' Emma's own tone was perfectly even. But her own eyes signalled to Patrick that his message was received. He didn't believe her story. He thought she'd been battered.

'Will you help Ellen undress, please?' he asked. 'I'd like to check that she has no other injuries.'

Ellen was reluctant. 'It was only my face I hit,' she said quickly.

But Emma swiftly countered and left her no choice. 'Doctor must check the rest of you, Ellen, if you fell down the stairs. There may be something you haven't noticed yet. It's often the case, when you're in shock.'

Emma watched Patrick's thorough examination. Ellen lay with scared eyes on the ceiling as his hands gently searched.

'No bones broken,' he said at the end of it, and helped her sit up. Then he added quietly, 'But those bruises on your chest and legs weren't made today, Ellen.'

Emma had already seen that it was so. A plethora of bruises covered her, their form and colour clearly declaring to the trained eye that they were of different dates.

Ellen's face was pale. 'No—I—I did them another time. I—I tripped in the yard.'

Patrick placed his hand on her arm. 'Won't you let us help you, Ellen?' he asked in a soft voice.

Emma thought it had almost done it. She saw the woman's eyes glisten with unshed tears. But the fear which stopped her from telling them was too strong. She shook her head. 'I dunno—I dunno what you mean.'

Patrick's eyes sought Emma's in another wordless communication. Almost imperceptibly, she nodded. Aloud she said, 'I'll help Ellen to dress now, Doctor. Mercurochrome on those cuts?'

Emma felt her way as gently as she could. Ellen seemed to feel relief that the doctor had gone, and opened up enough to tell Emma that she had four children and that her husband was out of work. She admitted that he drank. But she wouldn't say that it was he who had inflicted those bruises. Emma could guess at the threats that had been levelled at her to keep her silent, and didn't push. She merely set out to show Ellen that there was someone who cared about her, and that they would help her in any way she would let them. She secured a promise that Ellen would bring the children in for a check-up. Emma wondered if they were targets, too.

When she had gone, Cavanagh appeared in the treatment-room, his look intent. 'Any luck?' he asked.

Emma shook her head. 'Not really. Except that she did talk to me a bit. Four kids. Husband out of work and drinks. Not enough money. Not enough food. Debts. And she's scared.'

Patrick looked at her with grimness. 'With reason, it appears.'

She nodded. 'I asked her to bring the kids in. I think she will. I didn't press her—just tried to make her feel she had a friend.'

Patrick's face relaxed into a small smile. 'I'm sure you succeeded,' he said, and suddenly put his hand on her back. 'If anyone can win her confidence, you can.'

Emma's colour heightened at the compliment, and at the warm touch of his hand. 'I hope so,' she said a little breathlessly.

'Are the children well?' he asked.

'Th-they get a lot of colds, she says. And earaches.'

'Probably the result of poor nutrition.'

'Yes. She says the youngest isn't gaining weight.' Emma had a strange sense that they were talking at random as Patrick stood beside her, his hand still on her back. It darted through her mind that this was her chance to speak to him. She glanced up at his face, trying to read it, but it didn't tell her much. Save only that the fine hazel eyes met hers steadily, there was nothing in his expression to suggest that he would welcome talking of themselves. Once again, Emma's courage failed her. 'Well, I think that's it for the day,' she said, and Patrick dropped his hand.

'Yes. Thank you for your help,' he said formally. And then Anne had come to ask them if they were finished, and all conversation was at an end.

As she rode home on the bus, Emma cursed herself for her cowardice, and wondered about the significance of that gentle hand.

'Mrs Grady's first, Dr Cavanagh. I think all her test results are back.' Emma laid the papers at Patrick's

elbow on the following morning, but he didn't pick
them up.

He turned instead to Emma and startled her by saying, 'Why are you calling me that?'

Emma's heart gave a little thud. She didn't answer
immediately, and in the gap Patrick said, 'Need we be
so formal when there's not a patient present? It seems
a little silly. In the circumstances,' he added in a low,
wry voice.

'No. Of course, you're right. I don't know why
I——' she answered quickly.

'You don't have any objection to calling me Patrick,
do you?' he asked in a mildly sardonic tone.

'No. Of course not.'

'Or to my calling you Emma?'

The sound of it gave her a start. She had always
loved Patrick's voice. It was deep and resonant. No
one had ever said her name in a way that she loved
more. It flooded her with feeling.

'No,' was all she could manage at first. She felt
rather than saw Patrick's eyes on her face, her own
fastened on the papers she'd placed on his desk. Then
she said, 'I'm sorry. It is silly, of course. I suppose I
thought you might not want——'

'What?' His eyes seemed to draw hers up to him.
They met her grey ones straightly. His face was calmly
watchful.

'I can't explain it,' she ended helplessly. 'Shall—
shall I bring in the patient?'

There was a brief pause, then he said, 'Yes. Thank
you, Emma.'

As Emma did so, she tried to explain it to herself.
Partly it had been the result of his own formality. But
partly, too, it had been a device to keep her own
non-professional feelings at bay. She knew it hadn't

been working. She might as well give it away.

She began to call him Patrick, and by the end of the week was able to hear her own name on his lips with only the smallest speeding up of her heart. But she was no closer to being able to meet his eyes without an uncomfortable lurch of that unruly organ. Patrick, on the other hand, remained as enigmatic as on the first day.

CHAPTER FOUR

'WE'RE almost fully booked on Monday already,' observed Marje. 'Lucky we decided to leave some spaces every day for walk-ins.' She shut the appointments book at the end of the clinic's first week of operation. 'What are you doing at the weekend?' she asked Emma.

'Playing golf tomorrow,' said Emma. 'I don't know why I'm playing golf. I hate the game. It's the silliest, most frustrating pastime I've ever engaged in. I think I must have a strong streak of masochism.'

Emma's listeners laughed. 'I tried to play,' said Helen. 'I couldn't hit the ball at all.'

'Oh, I can hit it,' declared Emma. 'Into the sand-trap, into the lake, into the trees. . .'

They laughed again. 'Well, you have fun, love,' Marje told her. 'You've been looking a bit tired this week.'

'Fun is not what golf is for, Marjory,' Emma told her sternly. 'Golf is to remind you that, whatever awful job you do during the week, it's a better way to spend your time than golfing.'

There had been some truth in what Emma had said. She did find golf frustrating. But it was also a challenge, and that was what she needed this weekend—something so absorbing that she would have no time to think. After her second attempt to get out of the bunker on hole three, she began to think she'd chosen exactly the right thing. Her friend, Virginia, stood by, watching her and stifling giggles.

'What about a seven iron?' Virginia suggested.

'What about a shovel?' Emma replied, and Virginia laughed out loud. 'Thank you,' said Emma. 'Just what I need. Ribald laughter from the gallery.' Virginia giggled again, just as Emma brought her club down behind the ball. She hit it too flatly and it sailed right across the green into the bunker on the other side. Emma Treloar made a noise between a groan and a scream as Virginia Mason collapsed in helpless laughter.

'I think you're improving, Em,' observed Virginia in the clubhouse later. She was a bigger girl than Emma, with straight blonde hair tied back in a ponytail. Her face was warm and good-humoured, exactly the right sort of face for a social worker. She worked at the hospital and for many years had been Emma's closest friend.

'True. There were some holes on which I missed the hazards, weren't there?' agreed Emma. 'I think I should score that way—not the number of strokes, but the number of hazards I land in. My score would still be higher than yours.'

Virginia giggled into her drink, but took a sidelong look at Emma. 'How was the rest of the week?' she asked gently, aware of her friend's situation.

'I'm attempting to stay out of the sand-traps,' Emma told her. She took a sip of her drink and gazed out over the rolling green of the golf course. 'I'm doing OK, Ginny. I'm doing my job—concentrating on the patients. He—he's always polite. But—that's all.'

'You still haven't spoken to him, then?'

'No. I—once or twice I thought I might. But—it's so hard to know what he's thinking. He's so remote.

Maybe he just doesn't care any more. Maybe he wouldn't want to hear it.'

'Emma! Maybe! You've got to know! Talk to him. This isn't like you.'

Emma gave a wry smile. 'You mean you didn't know I was such a coward?'

'I mean I know you're *not* a coward,' said Virginia with emphasis.

'I think I am,' Emma said sadly. She raised her eyes to her friend. 'I don't think I could bear to hear him express polite regret that it happened, and tell me it's too late—that he doesn't care any more. And I'd have to work with him still. That would be unbearable.'

Virginia sighed. 'I see your point. But Emma, you have to know some time. If that's the case, will it be any better later?'

Emma knew she was right. Perhaps it would be worse.

If her round of golf had gone no more smoothly than it ever did, it had at least distracted Emma and provided her with some fresh air and exercise. And talking to Virginia had given her new resolution. Ginny was right. She must find out whether there was any hope for her with Patrick. She had to tell him what, in any case, he had the right to know. Even if he no longer loved her, she couldn't let him go on believing she had played him for a fool.

'How did the golf go?' asked Marje as Emma joined the others for their morning cup of tea in the staffroom.

'About as well as the Battle of the Boyne for the Southern Irish,' she said consideringly, and for the first time heard Patrick Cavanagh give an involuntary laugh. Her eyes instinctively went to him, but with an effort she controlled them and turned to face Marje

Gilbert. 'I did keep out of a few traps,' she conceded.

'You didn't win, then, love?' asked Marje.

'That could only happen if my friend accidentally drowned in a water hazard,' she explained. 'Then I would win by default.'

'Maybe you could push him in a water hazard,' Helen suggested.

Emma ignored the false assumption for the sake of the joke. 'I've thought of it,' she said.

'Emma, you did a good job with Ellen Fleet. She's brought the children in.' Patrick had come to the treat-ment-room. He leaned his tall frame against the door-jamb. 'The three youngest are all right. Malnour-ished, with colds and ear infections. The eldest is the problem. I think he's being abused. But he's not very keen to have me examine him.'

'Can I help?' asked Emma.

He nodded. 'I think you can, if you don't mind.'

The little group waiting in Patrick's consulting-room was one of the sorriest families Emma had seen. Ellen Fleet was there, looking anxious and pale. But hers was nothing to the pallor of three little boys and a skinny little girl. They stood silently, in ragged, rather dirty clothes, shrinking against their mother, with their eyes on the ground. The girl, a toddler of two, was crying in a miserable kind of way, half-heartedly, as though she had already learned in her short life not to hope for much in the way of comfort. The eldest boy was about seven, and stood slightly apart, looking scared.

Emma clasped the mother's shoulder. 'Hello, Ellen. I'm glad you've come.' The woman gave her a thin, pathetic smile. 'Now, who have we here?' Emma greeted each child as Ellen gave her their names. The eldest was Joey. Emma bent down before him. 'Hello, Joey. How old are you?'

The child flicked his eyes up to her apprehensively, but seemed to see nothing to alarm him in the pretty face with the smiling grey eyes. He swallowed and said, 'Seven.'

'Oh. You're a big boy, then.'

He seemed to consider this, and finally nodded.

'Do you play footie?' Emma took it slowly, asking him questions that might interest him and that he could easily answer. But it wasn't easy to make contact with this wary child. She had almost despaired of finding common ground when she asked him what he wanted to be when he grew up, and she saw the first flicker of animation in his pinched little face as he said he wanted to be a jockey.

Emma thought swiftly. 'Well, isn't that funny?' she said. She waved her hand in Patrick's direction. 'Dr Patrick wanted to be a jockey, too!'

Joey Fleet turned his eyes towards Patrick Cavanagh's six-foot-something, thirteen-stone frame, and finally there dawned on his face the ghost of a grin. 'Gawd,' he said. 'It 'ud 'ave ter be a big 'orse!'

Ellen said, 'Joey!' but Patrick had thrown back his head and given a shout of laughter.

He grinned back at Joey ruefully. 'Yes, I'm afraid you're right, Joey. I—er—had to give the idea up when I kept getting bigger. I decided to be a doctor instead.'

Joey gave Patrick a look of kindly sympathy. 'Oh, well,' he said, 'I s'pose that'd be orright, too.' He clearly didn't think it was nearly as good.

'If you're going to be a jockey, Joey, you'll have to be very strong and healthy,' Emma said. 'Isn't that right, Patrick?'

Patrick nodded. 'Yes. It takes a lot of strength to control a horse.'

Emma put a hand on the child's arm. 'Why don't you let Dr Patrick take a look at you? So you can be sure to grow up fit and strong.'

Joey glanced at the doctor. It seemed to hang in the balance for a moment. Then, as though convinced against his will, he gave a reluctant assent. 'Orright,' he said.

Emma led him up to the couch and helped him take off his shirt, as Patrick came to stand beside her. As she saw the boy's chest and back, Emma almost gave a gasp. He was covered in welts and bruises. Emma's eyes flew up to Patrick's, her lips parted in dismay. He stepped closer to her and with his back to Ellen gripped her hand in a steadying grasp. Emma shut her mouth firmly and took a few deep breaths. In a few moments, she looked back at Patrick to show him that she was under control. The hazel eyes scanned hers, then, seeming satisfied, he slowly let her go.

At the end of the examination, Emma helped the child to dress. Patrick sat down in his chair, and waited till Emma returned Joey to his mother's side. Then he simply said quietly, 'Ellen, this can't go on any more.'

Ellen Fleet was still and pale, and kept her eyes on the floor.

The doctor continued. 'Joey has healing fractures of his clavicle—collarbone—and humerus. He's lucky he doesn't have more.' Ellen was still silent, and Patrick's eyes sought Emma's in a quest for help.

Emma slowly came to Ellen's side, and put an arm around her shoulders. 'Ellen, are you so afraid of him?' she asked gently, and finally Ellen began to cry.

One thing they understood from the mother's

anguished sobs. He had said he'd kill Joey if she ever told.

Emma sank into a chair in the staffroom and gave a sigh compounded of sadness and relief. Patrick filled the teapot himself from the urn and stretched to relieve his tension. He put the pot and two cups on the table, and took a chair himself. It had taken a long time to do what they must for the Fleet family, and they had missed their lunch. The welfare agency had been notified as it had to be, and Ellen and the children had gone to a women's shelter in a nearby suburb. Just comforting Ellen had taken most of the time.

They talked of it for a while. 'Poor little man,' said Emma, and Patrick nodded.

'Brave little man,' he observed. Ellen had told them that Joey tried to stop her husband from hitting her. 'He'll make a good jockey.' Patrick's mouth suddenly curved in a little smile. 'As for the idea of my being a jockey, Sister Treloar, I'm surprised even a seven-year-old could swallow that.'

Emma found herself grinning back. 'Yes,' she said. 'Poor horse!'

Patrick gave a choke, and took a sip of his tea. When he looked up again, his face was once more serious. 'Where have you worked for the past year?'

Just the personal nature of the question had the power to make Emma tense, but she consciously relaxed herself and answered, 'Over the road. I stayed in Casualty till this place got to the active planning stage.' She saw him nod, and was glad he'd asked. It gave her the opportunity to ask about him. 'What were you doing?'

'Working for Médecins Sans Frontières,' he answered. 'Africa.'

So that was it. Not Community Aid Abroad at all, but another organisation that provided medical aid to under-developed countries. Why hadn't she thought of it? A sharp pang of regret stabbed at her. If she'd thought of that it could all have been different.

'What made you give that up?' she asked.

Patrick took a long while to answer. 'That sort of work—it isn't something one can do forever. I can't, anyway. One becomes—tired, overwhelmed. I saw this job advertised.' There was a pause, as though he might say more but couldn't think how to put it.

'I remember—you liked to work with these sorts of people,' Emma supplied.

'Yes,' he agreed. 'Because the system by-passes them. It ignores their needs.' There was a little silence again, then he asked, 'What else have you been doing?'

Emma wasn't sure how to answer. I've been searching for you and grieving for you, she thought. That was not what he wanted to hear. There was really nothing much else to tell him. 'I've been learning to play golf,' she said out loud.

Again a silence hung between them. Patrick was leaning forward, gazing into his teacup. Then he raised his head, seemed about to speak again for a moment, but only closed his mouth once more and returned to studying his tea.

Emma was conscious of a new sort of tension. Whether it came from him or her or both of them she couldn't have said. She knew her own mind was full of what she wanted to tell him. But this wasn't the time. There were patients waiting, and too many people around.

'What was it like in Africa?' she asked instead.

Patrick looked up and made a wry face. 'It would

take a long time to tell you,' he said, then added, 'I'd like to. You'd be interested.'

'I'd like to hear,' she said as evenly as she could.

Patrick's eyes seemed to search hers, then whatever he might have replied was lost when Marje came to tell him that there was a little boy just arrived who couldn't breathe too well.

Spring appeared to be on its way this week, and the resulting rise in the pollen count was playing hell with people's asthma, hay fever and other allergic complaints. A number of times now patients had sat gasping in the treatment-room, being given medication by face mask for their asthma. Some of the patients, esecially the small ones, didn't care for it at all.

'No! No!' sobbed a child's voice from the treatment-room, bringing Emma in to see if she could help Patrick. Besides the child's protests, she could hear also the wheezy breathing of severe asthma. She knew the child needed to be calmed quickly, or things could get rapidly worse. Emma didn't know the child or his mother, who was trying with Patrick to persuade him that the mask wouldn't hurt him.

This child, a pale four-year-old, wasn't having any. 'No-o-o!' he screamed, struggling to break free. To Emma's experienced eye, Patrick, beneath his calm, looked concerned.

'Hello!' Emma called. 'What are you doing on our spaceship?'

It was sufficiently unexpected to silence all three protagonists in the little drama. It gave her a chance to go on. Advancing into the room she asked, 'Is this a new astronaut? You didn't tell me we had a new astronaut, Major Patrick.'

Major Patrick, rapidly gathering his wits, managed to reply, 'Er—no. Sorry, Captain Emma.'

'Are you a new astronaut?' Emma asked the boy.

Benjamin Brown had been watching her with his mouth open. Now he closed it and nodded.

'Oh, that's good,' said Emma. 'We need a new astronaut. Are you coming to the moon with us?'

A glint of decided interest came to Benjamin's eyes. He nodded again.

'Good,' said Emma. 'Is this another astronaut?' she asked, indicating his mother.

Benjamin gave a little giggle and shook his head. 'That's Mummy,' he explained.

'O-o-oh,' said Emma. 'Is Mummy coming to the moon with us?'

Benjamin gave a wheezy laugh. 'No,' he said, as though she'd said something silly.

'No,' Emma repeated. 'Of course not. That was silly of me. Only astronauts can go, can't they? Only Major Patrick and Captain Emma and Captain Ben.'

'Am I Captain Ben?' he asked, looking excited.

'Of course you are. Well, I think it's time we set off. Do you want to kiss Mummy goodbye?'

Ben nodded enthusiastically and held out his arms. 'Goodbye, Mummy,' he said with the utmost cheerfulness. The young mother, to whom he'd been so desperately clinging till moments ago, kissed her little space explorer goodbye with a rather stunned air. But she hurried from the room with every appearance of relief.

Five minutes later, three astronauts sat side by side at the controls of their rocket. On the examination couch in front of their chairs were lined up the impressive dials of the diathermy machine, electrocardiograph and a machine used to shock people back into life when they'd had a cardiac arrest. All three, as was proper at take-off, had oxygen masks on their faces.

One, however, was plugged into the nebuliser and as they hurtled through space was receiving badly needed treatment for his asthma.

'There it is!' cried Captain Emma. 'The moon! Do you see it?'

'Yes!' cried Ben excitedly, peering ahead with the eyes of childhood. His next comment, in its very prosaicness, severely threatened the self-control of the larger astronaut on his left.

'Darn!' he said. 'I forgot my camera!'

Patrick sank back into his chair after saying goodbye to Ben and his mother and gave way at last to his feelings. When he had finished laughing and could speak again, he looked up at Emma, a smile hovering still at his mouth. 'I'd forgotten your talent for that sort of thing.'

Emma looked back at him with her impish smile, her grey eyes dancing. 'I did enjoy it, didn't you? Especially shooting down Darth Vader's spaceship— that was the best bit.' Patrick laughed again as Emma began to tidy up the treatment-room. 'The only problem is I have a feeling Major Patrick may tire of this game before Captain Ben. I do feel that Captain Ben will be expecting another intergalactic voyage when he comes back tomorrow.'

'Yes,' agreed Patrick. Something in his tone made Emma glance back at him. He was sitting still in his chair, but his smile had faded. A curious expression had taken its place as he watched her.

'Don't worry,' Emma said. 'We can always tell him that Major Patrick has been kidnapped by Darth Vader's men in revenge, and that our mission is to find him.'

Patrick's smile returned briefly, but it wasn't as it

had been before. 'Of course,' he said in a strangely
tight voice. 'Why didn't I think of that?' Emma waited
for him to say something else, but he only sat in his
chair, unsmiling again, and staring in front of him.

She wondered whether he was worried about the
boy. 'He'll be all right, won't he?' she asked.

Patrick seemed to rouse himself. 'Oh, yes,' he
replied. 'The nebuliser helped. And he won't be afraid
of using it now.' He rose to his feet, and smiled at
her. Emma thought he sounded awkward as he said,
'You were very helpful. As always.' Then he left to
get on with his work.

'Are you going, now, Emma?' Marje asked as she
packed up her bag at the end of the day.

'No, Marje. I'll be a while. Don't worry. I'll lock up.'

Patrick was seeing his last patient. Fiona Whitely
was finished, and Helen had already dashed out of the
door. Emma waited in the treatment-room, wiping the
benches in a desultory way, her mind busy. She
couldn't decide whether Patrick had been making a
tentative move towards her earlier, when he had
expressed a desire to tell her about Africa, or whether
it had just been the desire to catch up natural to old
acquaintances. The odd expression that had come to
his face after Ben had left also exercised her mind.
With Ben she had seen him more nearly as he had
been in the past than at any moment since he'd come
here. Playing a game for the benefit of a child, smiling
and laughing with her—that was the old Patrick
Cavanagh.

Ginny was right. She had to speak to him soon,
before she let her hopes rise any higher. Because she
was still hoping, she realised. She had decided. She
would do it tonight, as soon as he'd finished. As she

worked to fill in time, she tried to imagine the words she was going to use, and found her mouth already uncomfortably dry.

She heard Marje and Anne leave, calling a last good-bye. She waited for Fiona to do the same, but she didn't go. Presently she heard the jug boiling, and knew that Fiona was making a cup of tea. Damn the woman! Didn't she have a home to go to? Why was she hanging around?

It wasn't long after Patrick's patient left that she found out. Her heart speeded up as she heard Patrick leave his consulting-room. She felt the muscles in her body tense. She had to do this, no matter how he responded. But part of her wanted to run away. His steps came up the hall, past the treatment-room and into the staffroom, where they checked for a moment, perhaps at seeing that Fiona was still there.

'A busy day,' she heard him say, and thought there was an awkwardness in his tone, as though he wasn't easy.

'I wasn't as busy as you, thank goodness,' Fiona told him. 'I'm sure it doesn't trouble you to be busy straight away, but I must say I'm glad of a little time to feel my way.' Patrick made no answer, and Fiona plunged on a little too rapidly into a speech which sounded rehearsed. 'I thought I'd wait and offer to buy you a drink to celebrate the opening of the clinic. There's quite a nice pub on the next corner.'

Emma heard Patrick say, 'Ah!' and a split-second pause ensued before he continued, 'I'd like to do that, but—ah—Prudence will be expecting me.'

'Oh. I see.' Fiona's voice strove to hide her disappointment. 'Prudence is your wife?'

Again there was a tiny pause before Patrick Cavanagh replied, 'My companion.'

'Oh. Well. Some other time, then,' said Fiona.
'Well, I'll push off, then. Goodnight.'

Emma heard Fiona's high heels tapping away down
the hallway. Behind the half-closed door of the treatment-room, she stayed where she was. The tap in the
kitchen ran, and after a short time a glass made a clink
as it was replaced on the sink. Patrick was having a
drink of water. Finally his tread passed the door again,
but Emma made no attempt to stop him and speak.
She couldn't have. For Emma Treloar had sunk on to
the stool in the corner, and was silently crying. She
wouldn't speak to him at all now. She'd never explain.
For, after what she had just learned, there wasn't
any point.

'Don't you annoy me,' warned Emma. 'I've had the
rottenest day you can imagine.'

Tiger, with his scarred coat and the tattered right
ear hanging over his face at a rakish angle, looked as
though he could imagine some rotten days, but he
forbore to comment, and only waited resignedly beside
the refrigerator for her mood to soften.

She dumped the bowl of cat food in front of him at
last, and he miaowed apologetically before tucking in
as if to say he was sorry, but a cat still had to eat.

A person ought to eat, too, Emma knew, but she
didn't feel like it.

That was that, she thought—the end of a dream.
Prudence. 'My companion'. She oughtn't be surprised.
It ought to have occurred to her that he might be
married. So he was living with someone—it was just
the same. It boiled down to one thing—Patrick had
replaced her. His indifference was not feigned. He had
fallen in love with someone else. He would never live
with someone unless he had.

For a while all thought was once more suspended. Then, as she wiped her tears away with the back of her hand, there came the anguished questions. How could she have been so stupid as to let herself hope? Why, oh, why did he have to come to work at her clinic, of all the places in the world? And why hadn't she got over him as he had got over her?

They were questions without answers. She knew it was pointless asking them. She could only accept what a malign fate had dished out, and regret for the rest of her life that it had been her own hasty action that had set the train of events in motion. Patrick would never know now why she'd done it, but it didn't matter. There was nothing to be gained by telling him now that he was happy with someone else. It would only bring back sad memories. And it would make him uncomfortable if he were to guess that she still cared. That must be hidden from him.

She could not leave the clinic. It was her baby, her beloved project. Even had she not cared so much about working there, the explanations that would be required if she were to leave were too painful to contemplate. What could she say to Evan Thomas, to John Morrison, to the girls? What could she say to Patrick himself? No. She had to stay there. Somehow she had to accept what had happened, to accustom herself to the fact that he belonged with someone else now, and that they would never more be anything but colleagues.

'I'm sorry, Emmy,' said Virginia gently. She had called in out of some instinct on her way home from a meeting.

Emma attempted a smile, but it wasn't a very convincing one. 'You were right. It was better to know it now. It's just—going to be—a bit difficult for a while. . .'

There was a pause. 'You're not tempted to go out with anyone else?' Virginia asked, and Emma made a face.

'There's no one else I'm interested in,' she replied, and glanced at her friend when there was no answer. 'I know, Ginny. It's been fourteen months. But I don't think now is the time. And I really don't know anyone. . .'

'What about John Morrison?' Virginia asked gently. 'From what I gather he thinks you're the best thing since floppy disks.'

Emma managed a shaky laugh. 'He's a nice man. I like him. He's a good administrative officer. He was very helpful in setting up the clinic.'

'I bet he was,' said Virginia. 'Well?'

Emma shook her head. 'No, Ginny. Never.'

Virginia regarded her friend silently for a moment, then said gently, 'You know, Em, you'll never find anyone exactly like Patrick again. It'll have to be someone different.'

Emma smiled rather grimly. 'Don't I know it,' she said.

CHAPTER FIVE

EMMA woke in the morning feeling no better than when she had finally fallen into a fitful sleep. But she forced herself to eat a little breakfast and to appear at work behind a mask of composure. It didn't help that Patrick himself noticed her pallor and remarked on it in between the first two patients.

'Are you unwell, Emma?' he asked, surveying her with a professional eye. His tone was kindly.

It was the first time Emma had had cause to regret his acuteness. 'I've got a bit of a headache, that's all,' she said, endeavouring to stop further enquiry.

Patrick didn't appear to want to let it go. 'Do you get headaches?' he asked doubtfully.

Emma gave him to believe that she did sometimes, and he further tormented her by asking in a concerned way whether she had taken anything for it. Emma lied baldly to escape from a solicitude that threatened to overwhelm her.

She tried to immerse herself in her work. It appeared to her as the day wore on that the staff of Casualty at RPA were endeavouring to help her in this regard, since it soon became obvious that quite a lot of people, including minor trauma cases, were being diverted to them from there. The reason became clear when a cross father brought his seven-year-old daughter in.

'Just sit down there,' he ordered. 'And stop your crying. You brought it on yourself.'

Emma came forward to learn what had happened

to the child with a blood-stained towel pressed to her head.

'They sent us over from Casualty,' the father explained. 'There's people everywhere over there. They reckon there was a big pile-up on the expressway.' Emma immediately understood. In that case, Cas would be overflowing with people who needed help much more urgently than this child. 'She's a very naughty girl,' her father told Emma. 'She took her brother's bike, and of course she came off it. There's a cut on her head. Looks like it needs stitches, and serve her right. Might teach her a lesson.' Since this sympathetic speech served only to make the little girl sob more brokenly, Emma felt it might be wise to remove the child to the treatment-room straight away, and was pleased to encounter Patrick in the hallway as he said goodbye to his current patient.

He raised an enquiring eyebrow.

'Fell off her brother's bike,' said Emma briefly. 'Scalp laceration.'

Tracey Reid sobbed miserably the whole time Emma washed her wound and made her preparations for Patrick to suture it. On this occasion none of Emma's attempts at consolation seemed to help. Finally she was ready, the wound clean and covered with a sterile pad, and all the equipment set out neatly. She went to let Patrick know he could begin.

'Is her mother with her?' Patrick asked as he heard the child's crying.

Emma shook her head. 'Dad is, but he's too cross to be helpful. I'm afraid Tracey's in disgrace. He's in the waiting-room, scowling.'

'I see,' said Patrick drily as they entered the treatment-room.

A small girl for seven, Tracey presented a pathetic

picture. The blood was gone now, but she was pale and her head hung down, the tears plopping on to her skinny lap. Patrick seemed to consider a moment, then he picked up a chair and placed it in front of the one in which Tracey sat.

'Hello,' he said softly.

Tracey looked up and gave another sob. She didn't look frightened—only broken-hearted and ashamed.

'What's your name?' asked Patrick quietly.

'T-Tracey,' was the barely audible reply.

'Mine's Patrick,' he said. 'I'm a doctor. I'm going to fix your head.'

It won no answer, but she did look up for a second at his face.

'Did you fall off a bike?' he asked gently, and she nodded, weeping again. Patrick continued, his voice calm and low and infinitely gentle. 'Was it a very big bike?' he asked.

There was a pause, then Tracey nodded again.

'Was it a two-wheeler?'

Tracey looked up now and stopped crying, caught by the interest in his tone. 'Yes,' she gulped.

Patrick nodded, his face composed and kindly, his lips in a small smile. 'Did you get very far on it?' he asked at last.

Tracey looked back at him uncertainly, then seemed to decide he was different; he wasn't angry with her like Dad. 'Yes,' she said, with just a tiny inflexion of dawning pride. 'To Mrs Thompson's place.'

Patrick smiled warmly. 'All that way?' he said.

And for the first time Tracey smiled back, and began to wipe the tears away with her hand.

This it was a different Tracey who was returned to the care of her father with five stitches in her head. Even though Dad was still angry, he didn't have the power to make her feel as wretched as she had. For the doctor had thought she was very brave, and that she'd be a good bike rider when she was a little bigger. She understood she mustn't do it now—not till she was taller. The doctor had shown her how tall she was on a chart, and how tall you had to be to ride a two-wheeler safely. She knew she would have to wait. But she no longer felt so ashamed.

Emma cleaned up in the treatment-room, throwing the blood-stained swabs away and putting the used needles in the disposal bin. She didn't know why she felt worse than ever. He had been wonderful with the child—gentle and tender and understanding. So why was it so hard to stop herself from crying? Then Emma, as she thought about it more, began to realise. It was because he *was* those things—because he was as kind and loving as he had ever been, and because he was a man who could understand better than she could a little girl's pain.

A few tears escaped her control and welled over her eyelids. Emma was crying again for what could never be.

As early as the end of the second week, the clinic was beginning to have its regular customers. Emma judged that most of the people they'd seen in the last two weeks would return. The comments from the patients were universally favourable. The service was free; it was friendly and personal; and they didn't have to wait very long. They weren't just a number here.

Emma was glad. She felt that here they could do the job well, that for once in their lives these disadvantaged people were getting the sort of care they deserved. If it weren't for Patrick, Emma felt she'd be content. She did feel better at the end of the week than at the beginning, or at least she had more command of herself, and could make her customary dry comments as though nothing was the matter.

'Emma! Tea's ready,' called Marje, and Emma went to join the others in the staffroom. 'I bought some decent tea,' Marje told them. 'If I have to drink any more of that health department stuff my insides'll be addled.'

'It's not very nice, is it?' agreed Fiona Whitely.

'It's not tea at all,' Emma asserted. 'It's a by-product of the wood-chip industry.'

Fiona gave a little chuckle. She had relaxed a little since she'd come here. Emma found she was beginning to like her after all. Contrary to what Emma had expected, Fiona was quite good with the patients though she came from a very different social stratum. And the patients seemed to like her too.

'Where's that Dr Patrick?' Marje demanded, and was answered by his voice from the doorway.

'Present,' he said in a mild tone.

'I've poured your tea. It's getting cold,' she told him severely, and he meekly came to take it from her hand.

Emma thought Patrick was more like his old self with Marje than anyone. No one intimidated Marjorie Gilbert, and his cool reserve troubled her not a bit. Anne, too, had been won over by his unfailing courtesy and pronounced him, 'All right. Nicer than I'd thought'. Even Helen managed to chat with him easily enough in the lunch-hour now, though she still said she'd rather work with Fiona.

'Hey, Emma—are you going to the Cas party on Saturday?' Helen asked her.

Emma shook her head. 'No, I'm going to the mountains for the weekend.'

'Ooh. That sounds nice. A romantic weekend?' teased Helen.

Normally Emma would have made some dry rejoinder, but with Patrick present she couldn't stop herself from blushing, just as though Helen had hit the mark. 'I'm going to play golf at Leura,' she announced. 'Not content with punishing myself here, I'm going to drive a hundred miles to punish myself.'

Helen laughed. 'Well, at least you'll have a nice view.'

'I expect the sand-traps will look much the same there,' said Emma with an air of mournful resignation which made them all laugh except, she noticed, Patrick. He was regarding her, she thought, with an odd sort of scrutiny, for all the world as though he sought the answer to some question in her face. Her eyes met his for an instant, and his as quickly dropped away.

'Do you play golf, Fiona?' Helen asked, and she shook her head. 'You, Dr Patrick?' Like the receptionists, Helen used the title they tended to use with children for the doctors. Somehow they couldn't bring themselves to address him as 'Patrick'.

'I have been known to,' he answered, 'and I find myself much in sympathy with Emma. Except that water hazards seem to be my speciality.'

Emma couldn't help laughing. 'I think I'd prefer that,' she asserted. 'At least when it lands in the drink you can shrug your shoulders, walk away and start again with a new ball.'

'If you haven't tossed your clubs in after it,' he said quietly, and made them laugh.

'I've seen that,' said Emma. 'A man threw his whole golf bag in. When we came back down the next fairway, he'd gone away and come back with a mask and

snorkel and fished them out.' The others exclaimed.
'Yes. Poor fool, I thought. He can't help himself. He's
relented. But no. He simply recovered his car keys
from the pocket and chucked the bag back in.' They
all roared with laughter.

'Admirable fellow,' murmured Patrick.

'I thought so,' she said. 'He had my profoundest
respect.' She glanced up at him as she spoke, and saw
his lips curved in a smile that for once encompassed
his whole face. He stood in an attitude that brought
back a flood of memories. She'd forgotten that habit
he had when he was joking of standing with his head
erect and smiling down with his eyes. It had always had
a devastating effect on her and today was no different.
Emma thought she might have winced before the
onslaught of feelings, but she wasn't sure. All she knew
was that his smile had quickly fled, to be replaced
by another of the searching looks she'd encountered
before.

Emma pulled down the window sashes and fastened
them. 'I think we may need a fan in summer,' she
said. 'These old houses aren't very well ventilated.'

Patrick came out to hand the last patient's file to
Marje. 'We should approach Admin about that, I suppose?' he said, overhearing.

'You can leave that to Emma,' Marje remarked.
'She's got special influence.'

Patrick raised one eyebrow in a question, but Emma
silenced Marje with a minatory look. It was the opinion
of the girls, like Ginny, that John Morrison, the admin
officer, was in love with her. Emma, knowing it was
close to the truth, didn't want him made game of. She
liked John very much, though she had no romantic
interest in him.

'Phones switched off?' she asked Marje to prevent any further questions and answers.

'All ready to bolt out the door,' Marje told her. 'Tiger'll be waiting for you. We're a bit late.' The girls knew the story of the freeloading cat.

'He can keep waiting if he's dug up my petunias again,' she said darkly.

'A cat?' asked Patrick.

'Yes. He came with the house.'

Patrick nodded. 'I have one like that, too. The last tenants left it with me. Till they got settled in their new house, they said.'

Marje and Emma looked at him with silent pity.

'I know,' he said. 'I'm a sucker.'

They laughed.

'Do you have any other residents?' he asked Emma.

'A colony of mice,' she said. 'A few less numerous than at first, but only a few. Tiger's had a hard life. He says he's in semi-retirement.' She gave him a droll look, and saw him smile a little.

'I see. I'm not the only sucker,' he said.

'Not by a long chalk,' Emma admitted.

Patrick sat on the desk. He seemed to want to chat. 'Where do you live now?' he asked.

'Stanmore,' she told him, and he nodded.

'Semi-detached?' he asked.

'Yes. Quite a nice little Victorian terrace.'

There was a small pause before he asked, 'Two storeyed?' and Emma answered,

'Yes.'

Patrick nodded again, and fell silent, apparently inspecting his shoe. He made no attempt to get up and go home. Emma began to wonder. 'Do you drive to work, or take a bus?' he asked suddenly.

'Bus,' she said. 'I still haven't bought a car.'

He looked up at that, and opened his mouth as if
to speak again, then evidently changed his mind and
closed it.

Emma was puzzled. Was he trying to make polite
conversation? Or did he have some reason for asking
those things?

Patrick picked up the stapler from the desk and
toyed with it. 'Do you live alone?' he asked. 'Apart
from the livestock?'

So that was it. He was curious to know whether she
was with someone, as he was, and didn't wish to ask.
Emma schooled her face. 'Yes,' she said as casually
as she could. 'The cat, the mice and I make more than
a houseful.'

Patrick nodded and continued to play with the
stapler, but his eyes once more scanned her face in
quite the same way as they had done at lunchtime—
as though he was looking for something there. But this
time Emma understood it. Curiosity. Perhaps even—
give him credit—a desire to know whether she had
found happiness, as he had.

Emma was suddenly tense. She didn't want him to
ask whether her fictional romance had prospered.
What could she say about it? She was about to
announce that she had to go, when Marje, coming back
from putting the files away, spared her the necessity.

'You still here?' she asked, then, 'Dr Patrick—are
you wrecking my stapler?'

Wednesday was specially busy for some reason. Emma
guessed that it was extra busy in Casualty too, judging
by the number of people they had diverted to the clinic.
As the afternoon wore on there began to be a bit of
a wait—not, it was true, the sort of marathon delay
that people encountered across the road, but long

enough. Their customers waited patiently, used to far worse. One man who Emma thought didn't look too well, however, she took to the treatment-room to lie down until it was his turn.

'What's the trouble, Mr Blair?' she asked, intending to take a preliminary history.

'It's this darn indigestion,' he said, placing his hand on his chest. 'I never had it so bad before.'

Emma's expression didn't change. No one could have detected the sudden alerting reaction that spread through her body and brain. 'What is it like?' she asked him.

'Like someone sittin' on me chest,' he said. 'Like a weight, only it's a pain, too.'

'How long have you had the pain?' she asked, keeping her voice calm.

'Two—three hours. Never had it so long, neither.'

Sister Treloar didn't wait for Dr Cavanagh to finish with his patient. The doctor looked mildly surprised for an instant when she asked him to come staight away to another patient, but the wordless communication that had developed between them those years ago in Casualty, and of which they still seemed at times to be capable, sprang up again, and he excused himself swiftly and came.

'Fifty-two-year-old man with central crushing chest pain for three hours,' she told him as they made their way to the treatment-room. 'His colour's not very good.'

They both knew what it meant. This was no indigestion. Harold Blair, fifty-two-year-old father of three children still at school, was having a heart attack.

The man lay on the treatment-room examination couch, his face screwed up in pain. His face, as Emma had noted, was a grey colour, his skin damp with sweat.

Patrick moved quickly to his side and took his hand, his own fingers on the man's pulse. Emma, as swiftly, took a bottle of tiny tablets from the cupboard, and handed them to the doctor before he could ask for them.

'Harry—I want you to put one of these tablets under your tongue and let it melt there,' Patrick said. 'It may help with that pain.'

Harry Blair raised his head a little and reached out a trembling hand for the tablet. 'Thanks, Doc——' he started to say, but got no further. He didn't take the tablet. He fell back on to the couch, his right hand dropping limply at his side. Harry Blair was dead.

Perhaps one second passed before his attendants sprang into action—the second that it took the human mind to grasp the fact of a cardiac arrest. After that, however, there was no more hesitation. Doctor and nurse swung into operation like the interlocking parts of a well-oiled machine. They moved with lightning speed, as they knew they must if Harry Blair was to have another chance at life.

In a few seconds, Patrick had an airway in and a mask on his face, and Emma was pumping his chest. Emma had buzzed Helen and she was there in a moment, saying, 'Hell!' as she saw them, but going straight to work.

'Take over from Emma,' Patrick said, and she did so, leaving Emma free to help Patrick do what he must to re-start Harry's silent heart.

Task followed task smoothly, in an ordered sequence, with little speech. Emma and Patrick had done this together before. They had no need to talk. A tube slid into Harry's trachea, an intravenous line into his vein; electrodes were placed on his chest to pick up any impulses, to tell them whether his heart was doing anything, the result displayed on a screen. The trace on the monitor was a straight line.

'Adrenalin,' said Patrick, and Emma had it ready. She squirted it from its syringe into Harry's vein as Patrick continued to press the bag that was delivering oxygen to Harry's lungs.

They watched the monitor, and felt the first stir of hope as an uneven, shaky series of undulations replaced the flat line. Ventricular fibrillation. It wasn't good enough. Harry's heart was moving now, but only in a quiver, not in a way that would give him back his life.

Emma had already charged the defibrillator, and had reached for the paddles even as Patrick said the word. They waited for the trace to strengthen to the coarse sort of fibrillation that would respond to a shock. 'Three hundred joules,' he added, and she nodded as she applied the paddles to his chest. It wasn't to be. As they watched, the waves on the screen subsided back to that ominous line. Harry wasn't going to make it easy.

'Repeat the adrenalin,' Patrick ordered in a voice devoid of emotion, and in the same calm way Emma did as he said. Once more Harry's heart obeyed its chemical command, and once more stopped again before the shock that might save him could be delivered to his chest.

'Give some bicarbonate, then more adrenalin. Then we shock on the first sign of a rhythm,' said Patrick calmly. 'Any rhythm.'

She did it. Sodium bicarbonate and adrenalin coursed into Harry's veins and made their way to his heart, circulated by Helen's regular compressions on his chest. The line on the monitor fluttered again, and Emma darted in, the electrical paddles in her hands.

'Go!' said Patrick, and she hit the button. Harry Blair's inert body jumped with the force of the shock. Three pairs of eyes focused on the monitor, and saw the straight line convulse, curve up, go flat again, then seemingly struggle agonisingly into a broken series of peaks that finally made the monitor sound. Beep, beep. . .beep. . .beep, beep. Three people waited, scarcely breathing, their whole beings concentrated on the green-lit screen, as the forces of life and death waged their war in the chest of Harry Blair.

It happened suddenly as it always did. The trace on the monitor, from a series of halting irregular spikes, burst out of its lethargy into the strong, even uniformity of glorious sinus rhythm.

Beep. . .beep. . .beep. . .beep. . .beep. The machine sang its song of triumph, its music dearer to the ears of its listeners than any they had heard. The three helpers breathed again, and so did Harry Blair.

It was, of course, not over. There was work still to be done. No one would make the smallest show of celebration till all had been accomplished to make Harry's hold on life secure. But soon Helen was no longer needed, and she gratefully slipped away to call the ambulance that would take the patient to Coronary Care. Still Patrick and Emma worked silently, Patrick speaking only to reassure Harry when he became conscious once more. When the ambulance arrived they were ready, Harry able to speak to them, his pain gone, his heart stabilised by the further drugs they had given him into a steady beat.

Only then, when Harry Blair was wheeled out of the door and down the hallway, out of their care, did emotion come to the fore. Then, as always, it welled up in them, what they hadn't had time to feel before. Emma saw the door close on the stretcher and let out a long pent-up sigh. She glanced up at Patrick, the relief spreading over her features and turning her mouth up in a grin. 'Phew!' she said.

Patrick looked down at her, his own dawning smile broadening in answer. And in a moment he'd done what he would have fourteen months ago. He'd reached out an arm and pulled her against his side. He pressed her there warmly, his chin resting against the top of her head. 'Nice triage work in Cas,' he murmured, and Emma burst out laughing, her body shaking in his arms. 'I presume Cas sent him here?' he asked.

'Yes,' said Emma, 'and I'm going to kill them.'

Patrick laughed at that. Emma felt the reverberation of it in her body, resting against his chest. A sudden terrible, wonderful feeling seized her—a tense, sweet hotness that invaded every limb. She stopped breathing, and felt at the same time Patrick's arms tighten their grip. They stood there for an eternal moment, both now silent and still. She felt him take a breath for which he seemed to struggle, then he dropped his arms and took a hasty step back. Emma turned blindly away, her senses reeling. What had they been doing, standing there like that?

The treatment-room clock ticked loudly in the stillness. Emma struggled to think straight, and her eyes fell on the disarray of the room. Her mind clutched at it as if at a life-raft. 'What a mess!' she said in slightly shaking voice.

Patrick focused on it, too. 'Yes. Looks as though a bomb's gone off,' he said tightly, and added, 'I'll help you clean up.'

'No!' said Emma too quickly. 'No—it's OK. You still have a patient. Go—go back to her. I'll do this.'

Patrick stood for a moment as though undecided, as

Emma stooped to pick up an empty syringe. She didn't look at his face. At last he said, 'All right,' and, after a pause, said softly, 'Thank you.' Then he went away.

CHAPTER SIX

IT WAS a long time before Emma returned to order. She had the room straight first, her own heart still trotting along at an abnormal pace. What on earth had they been doing? But even as she asked it again she thought she began to see. It had been so like those times in Casualty. They had worked together just as they had then, attuned to each other as if the past fourteen months hadn't been. And even after it was over they hadn't been able to return all at once to the present. They'd acted as though they existed for the moment in a time-warp, back in that period when those actions would have been as natural as breathing. Just in that way would he have hugged her to him then. And made a light remark to make her laugh. And just in that way would she have rested against his solid strength, taking pleasure in the feel of him and in his loving warmth.

Emma almost groaned aloud. The old love and the old desire had taken hold of her as he'd held her in his arms. But she mustn't have those feelings now.

She thought for a moment of how his arms had tightened, and wondered for a breathless instant if he could possibly have felt it too. But it couldn't be. He'd built up a life with someone else. If he had felt something, it was only the stirring of a memory. Or it had merely been a stiffening in dismay at the situation into which old habits had betrayed them.

Emma resolved to be sensible and think of it no

more. It would never happen again. The time-warp was gone.

'John's here,' Marje said to Emma, putting her head round the open door of the treatment-room. 'I'll give him a cup of tea.'

'Thanks, Marje,' Emma called, looking up from the plaster she and Patrick were doing. 'We're almost finished. This is the last, isn't it?'

'Yes, thank goodness,' Marje replied. 'What a day!'

Emma held the patient's arm up for Patrick to put the finishing touches to the job. They'd worked together silently for the rest of the day. Emma had kept her eyes and mind on her patients, only feeling rather than seeing at times that Patrick's gaze had fallen on her face.

'That's it,' Patrick told the patient. 'Just keep the arm in the sling for two days till the swelling goes down.'

Emma adjusted the sling, gave him a printed sheet about taking care of the plaster and cautioned him to come and have his circulation checked on the following day.

John Morrison's face lit up with the smile that always betrayed him when Emma joined him in the staffroom. Awkwardly, a little embarrassed, Emma introduced him to Patrick, who'd poured himself a cup of Marjorie's tea.

'How was your day?' he said to Emma.

'Terrific!' she said. 'We had a cardiac arrest.'

John Morrison's good-humoured face screwed up in horror. 'Lord!' he said. He was a pleasant-looking young man, about twenty-eight, of medium height and with dark blond hair. His eyes were blue and gentle. Everyone liked him. 'I'm glad we gave you that defibrillator,' he said. It had been a subject of debate. Defibrillators were expensive.

Emma nodded. 'So is the patient,' she said.

'Was the patient OK?' he asked, and looked relieved when Emma said yes. John had a degree in hospital administration. He wasn't a doctor. Tales of medical horror still made him shudder, even after some years of experience.

Emma poured herself some tea and sat down at the table with John and Patrick.

'Got everything else you need?' John asked, looking at Patrick as well as Emma. This was ostensibly what he'd come here for.

Patrick answered. 'I'm surprised at how well-equipped the place is. I didn't expect to find it half as good.'

'That's Emma's doing,' John said warmly, and gave her a smile in which the state of his heart was revealed for all to see.

Emma felt herself blushing. She had told John gently that she wasn't interested in romance. She liked him too well to put it more bluntly than that. But she wondered if one day she'd be forced to take a stronger line. 'That's not true,' she said aloud. 'We'd be nowhere without you, Johnno.' She couldn't suppress a smile. They sounded so much like a mutual admiration society. Well, it wouldn't hurt if Patrick thought that was how it was. It might stop him becoming aware that she still had feelings for him. 'There is one thing we may need, John,' she told him. 'A ceiling fan. In the waiting-room. I think it's going to be rather airless in summer.'

'I'll get it,' John said smilingly. 'I might have to steal the money from some other department's budget.'

Emma gave her most impish smile. 'Make it Cas,' she said. 'After today, they owe us.'

John gave his good-natured laugh. 'I can probably do that,' he said. 'What kind of fan? One like mine? With winter controls as well as summer?' He meant the one in his office. 'They don't cost much more.'

Emma grinned again. 'In that case, yes.'

John Morrison reluctantly got up to leave half an hour later. 'I've got a meeting,' he said, and gave Emma a small hug in parting as was his habit. 'See you later.' He gave Patrick his hand.

Emma and Patrick sat for a while longer, finishing their tea. 'I see it's true, then,' Patrick observed. 'You do have special influence with Administration. I wondered how we came to have such an expensive item as a defib.' His eyes flicked up at her, their clear hazel holding an odd expression. They seemed to Emma to hold a degree of puzzlement. Or perhaps disquiet. Or both. 'He's a nice chap,' he said quietly. 'I remember him from before.'

Emma, her colour up a trifle, nodded. 'He's an awfully nice chap,' she agreed. She had kept her voice even, but she could do nothing about her colour, and she saw Patrick's gaze sweep her face and take it in.

Again there was on his face that strange expression, as though something baffled him. He seemed to study her a moment longer, then looked away. 'I'd better be off,' he said at last. Slowly, as though the events of the day had wearied him, he got to his feet and left.

In the days after Harry Blair's cardiac arrest, Patrick seemed somehow different to Emma. He'd been quiet since he came here, but now he seemed if anything quieter. He seemed wrapped for the most part in an

impenetrable cloak of reserve, or perhaps it was a kind
of abstraction. A couple of times, she noticed, he didn't
seem to hear what someone had said to him. He looked
as though there was something on his mind. At times
he looked even sad.

Marjorie had remarked on it. 'You're looking
gloomy, Dr Patrick. Your cat died or something?'

Patrick had given a wry smile at that. 'No. The damn
thing's alive and well.' Emma thought he had stirred
himself to appear more light-hearted. 'It's being
courted by all the neighbourhood romeos. If I look
limp it's because I've been awake half the night listening to it being serenaded.'

'It's a she, then,' Emma observed, and he'd given
her a small smile.

'Yes. And as much trouble as the rest of her sex.'

It was greeted with howls of protest, which he'd
known it would be. But Emma thought there had been
a note of pain beneath the banter. It occurred to her
to wonder suddenly whether there was trouble between
him and Prudence. Emma couldn't stop a small feeling
of hope arising within her. She chastised herself for
this. What kind of love was it that would wish suffering
upon its object? For if that were the reason for
Patrick's seeming melancholy, it obviously mattered
to him.

It was her own feelings that troubled her when they
worked together. Rather than receding with time, since
Harry Blair's heart attack it seemed they had recurred
with a vengeance and were always waiting, ready to
be fanned from a smouldering glow into a flame of
emotion at any contact.

There was plenty of opportunity. Helen still wouldn't
swap with her—Emma had canvassed it subtly. Every
day was spent in casual and sometimes close contact

with Patrick. And now he didn't show the same repelling indifference. As quiet as he was, she now saw in his face and eyes a normal sort of human responsiveness in place of the earlier stone-wall blankness. It was as though their contact after saving Harry had re-established their connectedness. He would never love her again, but he could respond to her as a human being, perhaps as a friend. The thought of being Patrick's friend filled Emma with a peculiar sort of pain that only made being with him every day harder.

'There's a little old lady in the treatment-room with Patrick,' Anne said as Emma arrived at the clinic. 'She fell down the steps of the bus.' Emma left her bag in the staffroom and went to help him.

He looked up as she came in and said, 'Here's Sister Treloar. She'll give us a hand. This is Mrs Springer.'

A lady of some eighty summers lay on the couch, dishevelled and shaken. Patrick held her right forearm in his hands and Emma could see it was broken. 'A Colles',' she said, and Patrick nodded. It was the name of the fracture, just above the wrist. 'Can we fix it here?' she asked.

'Let's,' said Patrick.

He was right. If they sent her to Cas she'd be lucky to have it done by lunchtime. Emma could walk across the road with her later for an X-ray.

'Good,' said Emma, and began to make the preparations while Patrick explained simply what would happen.

'I feel such a nuisance!' said Mrs Springer, and embarked once more on the story of how it had happened. Emma knew she needed to tell it. She listened as she assembled the things they would need, interspersing sympathetic questions. Mrs Springer seemed to feel much better at the end of her recital, and was

even able to make a feeble joke. 'It must have been
the black cat that crossed my path yesterday.'

'Was it a bold-looking creature?' asked Emma. 'With
lipstick and false eyelashes, and followed by six tom-
cats? That's Dr Cavanagh's cat,' she asserted.

Mrs Springer was surprised into laughter.

Across the room, Emma saw Patrick grin. 'My cat
is not black,' he announced sternly, then added, 'She
was right in the other particulars,' and made the old
lady laugh again.

'What colour is your cat?' asked Emma. This sort
of thing was good for a patient. It took their mind off
a threatening procedure while you got ready for it.

'My cat is brown,' said Patrick with dignity.

'Brown?' Emma said. 'What sort of cat is brown?
Cats aren't brown. Dogs are brown. Are you sure it's
not a dog?'

Mrs Springer was laughing fit to burst something.
But she managed to gasp, 'Tortoise shell! Doctor probably means tortoise shell, dear.'

'You're right, Mrs Springer. I think I do. My cat is
tortoise shell. And we're ready to give you some local
anaesthetic so it won't hurt you at all when we set
that arm.'

She had forgotten about it for a few moments and
the laugh had relaxed her, but she looked a little anxious again now as he picked up the small needle. One of
Patrick's greatest attributes was his swiftness, thought
Emma, as she watched. For the little 'butterfly' needle
was in Mrs Springer's vein in a twinkling, and Patrick
was able to say, 'That was the only bit that hurts
at all.'

Emma wrapped the tourniquet round her upper arm
and in a few moments the old lady's forearm was full
of local anaesthetic, fed in through the needle in her

vein. Minutes later, she exclaimed as her arm became numb. Now came the part which, although it wouldn't hurt, was still alarming. Patrick and Emma had to pull the bones back into place.

'I'll hold the upper arm,' said Patrick quietly. 'You pull on the hand.'

To distract her, Emma once again resumed her attack. 'I don't believe you have a cat. I bet it's not a tortoise shell at all,' she said. 'I bet it's a dog.'

'It—is—not—a—dog,' said Patrick with emphasis as they began to exert a gentle pull.

'How do you know?' she demanded.

'It goes "miaow",' said Patrick.

'That doesn't prove anything!' exclaimed Emma. '*You* go "miaow". You just did.'

Mrs Springer burst out laughing again, as they pulled harder. There was a little give and they both felt the bones slide into place.

'Well done,' said Patrick. His eyes flicked up at Emma, full of a smile which had a lot of its old warmth. 'Another thing you're good at,' he said softly.

It disconcerted Emma. It wasn't the praise. It was the unexpected gentleness of his tone and the light in his eyes. Her heart speeded up and she felt a bitter-sweet confusion. She had trouble collecting her thoughts as they bent together to plaster the arm. She handed him the wrong-sized plaster, got her hand in the way and finally bumped his head with her own. 'Sorry!' she gasped.

Patrick turned his head to look at her, his face bare inches away from her own. For a few seconds his eyes met with hers, a question in them as though he wondered if something was wrong. Emma stared back, mesmerised by them. A tide of crimson flooded into her face. His eyes, perhaps seeing it, roamed her features for a moment, then came back to rest on her own. Only now something else dwelt at the back of them—a hard, fierce light that Emma couldn't begin to explain.

It had all taken seconds only. The next moment, their attention was back on the half-plastered arm. The only clue that it might have disturbed the doctor was in the finished product. It wasn't quite as smooth as the best plasters he'd done.

The rest of the day was no less disconcerting for Emma. Having got off balance at the start, it soon seemed to her that the patients were conspiring to keep her that way. Almost all Patrick's patients seemed to need her services. Her own, to her exasperation, needed him. At a time when Emma would have been glad to keep her contact with him to a minimum, they were constantly thrown together, sometimes close enough to touch.

It made her tense and nervous. Her awareness of him was heightened—of his face and eyes when they rested on her, of his body, of his deft, strong hands as he worked.

As the day wore on and became ever more trying, they both seemed to grow unaccustomedly clumsy. They got in each other's way, brushed hands awkwardly and once collided. Patrick put his hands on her upper arms to steady her. 'Sorry,' he said, giving her a rueful look. 'We seem to have lost our rhythm.'

They certainly had. And the feel of his hands on her had done nothing to help. They had two excisions booked in last thing in the afternoon. Both patients had moles that looked as though they were changing and needed to come off. They were running an hour late by the time they got to the first one. It was time for the rest of the staff to go home.

'You sure you don't want one of us to stay?' asked Marje kindly, but Emma shook her head. There was really no need.

Young Jodie Timms' mole was on her back and easy to remove. It wasn't long before Emma was holding out the little jar of formalin for Patrick to put it in. Old Mr Barnwell's was different. It was on the top of his ear. He lay on his side on the table, and Emma had to stand close to hold his ear forward for Patrick to get at it.

'That's it,' Patrick murmured beside her. 'Pull it down a little too.'

Emma watched him pick up the scalpel to begin, uncomfortable at their closeness but interested to see how it would be done in such an awkward spot.

'The only way to do this neatly is with a plastic surgery technique,' he told her. 'The incision will be this shape.' He sketched it with his scalpel-blade in the air. 'Then we can bring it together with stitches so that it will still look like a normal ear.'

Sid Barnwell chuckled. 'It don't much matter to me the shape of me ear, Doc,' he said.

Patrick grinned. 'We don't want it to look like I've chewed it off, Sid. It's not a good advertisement.'

Emma gave a ripple of laughter, then fell abruptly silent as Patrick moved closer to start the incision, so that his left arm actually rested against her own arm and shoulder. Her heart speeded up. She watched him begin, and did what he asked her, pulling the ear this way and that as he directed.

'That's it,' he murmured. 'Pull against me, Emma. Good.'

Emma had never seen the technique and found it fascinating. She was amazed at how well it came together when he'd removed the piece of flesh and begun to stitch it up. But it still wasn't enough to banish her feelings at the pressure of his arm.

'Just—that way,' he said, and put his hand on hers to show her which way he wanted her to hold it. As always the touch of his hand disturbed her, though it lay so lightly over her own. How was it that a touch like that could fill her with warmth and tension, and could make her heart accelerate again?

Keep your mind on the job, she admonished herself, and don't be so stupid. And then, in a moment, he was done. It was a nice piece of surgery, thought Emma. In a short time you wouldn't even notice the scar or the slight variation in shape. She had to admit it. Patrick was good at his job.

'Do you think you can get a dressing to cover that?' he asked, turning his head.

That was Emma's department. She nodded. 'I've got a stick-on that's just the right size.' She glanced up enquiringly. 'How long do you want it to stay on?'

Patrick stood looking down at her, appearing to consider the matter. He seemed to become distracted, however, and it took him a while to answer. When he did, his reply was halting. 'Ah—twenty-four hours. Then—leave it open to the air.'

Emma nodded, and gratefully moved away now to get the dressing. Patrick, she noticed, stayed where he was, staring unseeingly into mid-air. He hadn't moved when she came back with the dressing. Emma hovered for a moment at his side, wanting to get in to dress it. 'Shall I put the dressing on?' she asked finally, and he turned as though awakened.

'Yes. Sorry,' he said and stepped out of the way.

Emma returned to tidy up after seeing Sid to the door and found Patrick was already doing it. It was one of the things that the nursing staff in Cas had liked about him—that he didn't just walk away from the mess and leave it to them at the end of a procedure. He was one of the few who didn't.

'Thank you,' said Emma in acknowledgement, and went to scrub the instruments in the sink as Patrick disposed of the needles and blade. He threw the blood-stained swabs in the garbage and finally came to hold the lid of the sterilising tray for her while she placed the clean instruments in it. They both cast their eyes around to see all was tidy, and both spotted the swab on the floor at the same time. Both stooped at the same moment to retrieve it, then drew back saying, 'Sorry,' in unison.

It was too much for both of them. Emma started to giggle, and then to laugh as Patrick joined her. He looked down at her, his eyes alight. 'I'll toss you,' he said, and she gave another choking laugh.

'No. You have it. It's yours,' she said, her grey eyes dancing. 'You dropped it, after all.'

He grinned down at her. 'But you're closer to the ground than I am,' he said, and Emma gave a guffaw.

'I won't be when you're on your knees, Doctor,' she said, her mouth turned up cheekily, and Patrick gave a spurt of laughter that suddenly sounded a little hoarse.

He stood looking at her a moment, the laughter leaving his face. Emma felt her own desert her as an odd strained look came to his eyes. She became aware that her heart was pounding. She could hear it in her ears. She was staring at him and couldn't help it, for he was staring at her. And in his face was once again that fierce strange look, almost of pain.

Emma took an uncertain breath, and knew an urge to retreat. She took a step back, and said, 'I have to——' but got no further than that.

For Patrick had reached out a hand and taken her

by the wrist. Silently, with his eyes still on her, he
drew her close to him. They stood there, facing, close
together, his grip hard on her arm. Emma said nothing,
her brain whirling, her mouth slightly open in surprise.

Still he stood there, quite immobile, as though he
could neither go on nor go back. Still their eyes were
locked together, hers grey and wide, his intense, and
boring into her face. Then all at once he acted, as
though pushed over some brink. His arms encircled
her, slowly but strongly, and his lips came down
on hers.

And once again Emma knew she'd forgotten the
extent of what this man could make her feel. It came
back to her now in a dizzying instant as his mouth
moved sensually against her own. She gave a gasp and
felt his arms tighten, crushing her to his chest. At the
same time his kiss grew more fervent, his lips caressing
hers in a urgent, hungry quest. She could no more
resist him than fly. Already her lips had answered his
own, and her body had done so, too. Without knowing
she did it, her arms went about him and returned his
warm embrace. She clung to him, lost in the feeling,
her heart bursting with love and desire.

Emma knew that something was wrong—that this
was too good to be true. It was like a dream of something you'd longed for. You awoke and it hadn't
happened. But her mind at first couldn't wrench itself
free of the torrent of emotion the man had released.

His hands went up to her face then, and he held her
away for a moment, staring down into her eyes. That
was when it came to her, in that brief respite from his
embrace. He bent to kiss her again, but she put a
resisting hand against his chest. Unable to speak, her
breathing still disordered, she shook her head.

He stood still, looking at her, her face imprisoned

between his hands. His eyes were dark, their pupils enormous, a fire in their depths. He drew her face up to meet him again, but Emma found her tongue.

'No! Don't!' she gasped. It was almost a sob. 'W-we have to talk.'

Slowly he released her, his hands dropping to his sides. 'Yes,' he said.

Emma poured herself a glass of mineral water from the fridge, making silent enquiry as to whether he'd like some too. Patrick nodded. Wordlessly he had followed her to the staffroom and waited, perhaps as glad as Emma to have these silent moments to collect his thoughts. Finally, however, after drinking half a glass, she set it down and faced him across the table. 'You— still feel something,' she breathed, torn between hope and fear.

He was silent a moment longer, giving the tiniest wry smile. Then he nodded. 'And—you?' he said in a tight voice.

Emma swallowed. She nodded also, then was silent, her eyes down. 'But——' she flicked her gaze up to him again, steadfast and grave '—there's someone else,' she almost whispered.

Emma wasn't sure how to interpret the look in his eyes. They regarded her steadily, with a hard vigilance, probing the depths of her own.

His voice when he spoke was even and low. 'Is that an insuperable obstacle?' he asked.

His words stunned her. For a moment her brain didn't function. Then, as she grasped their import, a flush spread over her face. For she could only think that Patrick was sitting there offering to have an affair. It couldn't be true. Not Patrick. She must have misunderstood him.

Emma groped for a way to clarify what he meant.

'What—what do you want from me?' she asked.

'Whatever you want to give,' he said quietly, but there was a note to his speech as if he mocked her, or perhaps himself.

'What about——' Emma found she couldn't bring herself to say Prudence's name '—the other person?' she finished, a frown in her eyes.

There was no mistaking now the sardonic look on his face. 'I was two-timed once,' he said softly. 'I never knew.'

The words stabbed Emma like a knife. You did it to me, he was saying. Why shouldn't I do it to Prudence?

'Would you do that?' she asked in almost a whisper.

His answer was one word. 'Yes.'

'And—you think I would?' she said.

Patrick gave a wry half-smile that answered for him. You've done this sort of thing before, it said.

Emma shook her head slowly. 'You're wrong about me,' she said. She wanted to tell him how wrong, but she knew she could say no more. Already the tears were pricking at the backs of her eyes. Hastily she scraped her chair back and rose to her feet. He put out a hand as if to restrain her, but Emma evaded it and fled blindly from the room.

CHAPTER SEVEN

NEXT morning, for the first time, Emma considered seriously the possibility of leaving the clinic. Patrick had certainly changed, perhaps because of what she had done. The Patrick she had known in the past would never have cheated on a woman, nor offered her an affair. Emma had wanted him to say that he loved her, and that his other relationship was over, or shortly would be. She didn't want to share him, to be a 'bit on the side', to fill up the corners of his life. She had never been so hurt and angry.

It was difficult to greet Patrick as she had every other morning for the past few weeks. She thought a degree of strain was etched in his own face, too. Emma's heart lurched at the end of their morning tea, when he said simply, 'A word with you, Emma,' and indicated his consulting-room with a tilt of his his head. She had no choice but to do as he asked.

'Sit down. Please,' he said as he closed the door.

Emma did so. What did he want of her? Was he planning to renew last night's overtures?

Patrick sat down in his chair and gazed ahead for a moment, perhaps collecting his thoughts. Then his eyes came up to rest on her. 'I'm sorry,' he said with some difficulty. 'I oughtn't to have done as I did. Or said what I said. I want you to know there won't be a repetition. It was—sometimes—working with you. . .' His voice was constricted, and trailed away.

Emma knew only too well what he meant. It was hard to work all day together, to share touching and

anxious moments with the patients, and never to
acknowledge the feeling that she had for him. Now
that she knew some emotion towards her survived in
him, she could understand that he might feel the same.
It explained several moments that had puzzled her.
But it was harder for her, she thought, than for him.
She loved him. For him, it was not so serious—a case
of attraction, left over from before.

'What are we to do?' he asked. 'Would you like to
work with Fiona?'

Even though it was what Emma had wished herself,
she couldn't help feeling a little stab of hurt that he
wanted her to do so too. Irrational, she told herself.
It was the logical answer. Things were hardly likely to
be any easier between them now that they had shared
that kiss. How could they go on as they had, each
knowing that the other, at least with part of their
minds, would like to do it again?

On the other hand, how could they accomplish the
swap? Emma schooled her voice. 'That would be
sensible,' she agreed. 'I—had suggested to Helen
before that she might like to work with you—for a
change.'

Patrick gave a wry smile. 'Couldn't sell her the
idea, eh?'

'No,' said Emma frankly.

Patrick frowned. 'That makes it awkward.'

Emma nodded. 'I would have to—indicate that there
was a special reason for the change. Fiona would probably have to know, too.'

Patrick gave her a rueful look.

'Yes. I don't want that at all,' she said.

He gave a small sigh, and fell to inspecting his pen.
'I don't see what else is to be done,' he said finally.
'Except to—live with it.'

'I thought of leaving,' Emma said, and Patrick looked up quickly.

'No!' he said with force. 'This is your project. I won't have that. If we find we can't—deal with this, I'll leave.'

Emma's eyes flicked up to his. He looked as though he meant it. Her heart gave a painful squeeze. For all that it hurt her to be with him when he was involved with someone else, for all that his pass had angered her, the thought of his leaving again filled her with grief.

'It'll be all right,' he said gruffly at last. 'We're rational people. We can cope.'

Sister Treloar and Dr Cavanagh continued to work together and to give the patients their best. If the doctor again felt the stirrings of attraction when Emma smiled or worked close to him, he didn't give way to impulse and try to make love to her. And if his strong, handsome face and deep, gentle voice often filled her with unwanted emotion, she thought she managed not to let it show. There was a quietness, perhaps, about both of them. But in other respects they were outwardly normal, a well-matched, professional team.

Only occasionally the acutest observer might have detected a little hitch in their practised teamwork—an unplanned touching of hands from which both would withdraw with a little more haste than normal; or a certain fleeting look of regret when there had been some special contact of mind or heart.

The latter happened often. Emma found that she and Patrick still thought and felt alike as they had done from the first. She found herself wondering if it was like that for him with Prudence, and what his 'companion' did. Was she a nurse? Someone he'd met

abroad? It was on the tip of her tongue a few times
to ask him, but somehow she found she couldn't say
the woman's name.

'I've got a corneal foreign body for you to remove,
Emma,' Patrick announced, and Emma felt a familiar
shrinking. Foreign bodies—bits of dirt or metal—on
the cornea, the all-important clear part of the eye,
were commonly seen in Cas and general practice. In
remote areas, it was the sister who would often have
to remove them. Patrick had discovered Emma's reluc-
tance to touch patients' eyes back in Casualty, and had
tried to help her overcome her fear.

David Saunders, a young metal-worker, was already
lying on the couch when Emma came in. 'Sister
Treloar's going to remove that speck of metal, David.
She's got a very delicate touch.' Patrick stood at the
patient's head, a little to the left, and motioned for
Emma to take her place at his side.

Emma knew exactly why she hated this. The cornea
was about a millimetre thick. The grit was usually
firmly stuck, and had to be lifted off with the point
of a twenty-five-gauge needle. And there wasn't an
instrument sharper than that. Emma was always terri-
fied that her hand would slip or tremble, and that she
would plunge the needle through that thin barrier into
the eye.

Practice was the only thing that would make the fear
go away. Patrick had made her practise in Cas, knowing that one day she might need to do it alone. But
she still hadn't reached the point where she was
comfortable at it. She took her place with palms slightly
sweating, and dried them on her dress.

Patrick, turning a little towards her, gave her a quick
smile of encouragement as he saw it. 'Everything's
ready,' he said. 'I'll draw the bottom eyelid down for

FREE BOOKS CERTIFICATE

Yes! Please send me **Four FREE Temptations** together with my **FREE gifts.** Please also reserve a Reader Service subscription for me. If I decide to subscribe, I shall receive four superb new titles for just £7.80 each month postage and packing FREE. If I decide not to subscribe I shall contact you within 10 days. Any free books and gifts will remain mine to keep. I understand that I am under no obligation whatsoever - I may cancel or suspend my subscription at any time simply by contacting you. I am over 18 years of age.

7A4T

Ms/Mrs/Miss/Mr _____

Address _____

_____

Postcode _____

Signature _____

A FREE GIFT

Return this card and we'll also send you this cuddly Teddy Bear absolutely FREE.

A FREE GIFT

We all love mysteries, so AS WELL as your FREE books and Teddy Bear we've an intriguing gift for you.

MILLS & BOON READER SERVICE
FREEPOST
PO BOX 236
CROYDON
CR9 9EL

NO
STAMP
NEEDED

your hand still. I felt you—you held your breath for a good half-minute.'

Emma found herself flushing. Being held by you doesn't help to keep my hand still either, she reflected. Perhaps the thought could be read in her face, for he suddenly gave an almost bitter smile. 'You did very well. I'm sorry if I annoyed you.' With that he walked away.

'Hurry up, Emma. Get in the shower. It starts at six-thirty,' Helen called.

It was handy to work in a place that had once been a private house. It had a bathroom, and Helen and Emma had more than once used it to shower and change instead of going home when they were going out. Tonight they were going to an administration party. John Morrison had organised it and asked them both.

It hadn't been a good day to be going out afterwards. It was six o'clock by the time Emma had finished her work, and Patrick still had one patient to see. He would have to manage without her. Emma peeled off her uniform and stepped under the shower.

She had never been one to take an hour to dress, and she was ready before Helen even though she'd started late. Helen was still putting on her make-up in the mirror in the staffroom when Emma came to stand behind her, ready to go.

Helen glanced round. 'How do you manage to get dressed so quickly——' she began, then said, 'Hey, you look great!'

'Thanks,' Emma said somewhat shyly. She liked the dress she had on, but she had never been in love with her own looks.

Helen made up for her own lack of enthusiasm.

'That's a great dress,' she said, with a little envy. 'Your hair looks nice, too. You know I've never seen you with it down?'

It was true. Emma didn't wear it down very often. It wasn't convenient for work. A light, almost treacle-coloured brown, it hung in glossy curls to her shoulders, framing her slim face like a halo. Her dress was simple—a well-cut, form-hugging dinner number that came to a few inches above the knee.

'God, I wish I had legs like yours,' mourned Helen. 'I'd love to wear a dress that length.'

'I'd like your blonde hair,' Emma told her. 'Instead of indeterminate brown.'

'It's not!' protested Helen. 'It's a lovely colour. You know, you remind me of an angel with your hair like that—the ones in old paintings.'

Emma gave a very un-angelic shout of laughter. Patrick, coming to the staffroom after his last patient, was in time to see the angelic mouth turned up in its most impish smile. He stopped still in the doorway, and seemed uncertain as to whether to come in. His eyes ranged over Emma from the top of her shining hair to her shapely legs and feet.

'Oh, Dr Patrick!' Helen caught sight of him, and hastily put her make-up away. 'Come in. There's tea there. Are you going to the admin party?'

'I thought I'd look in later,' he said. He sauntered in and leaned against the sink.

Emma felt suddenly awkward. His eyes had returned to surveying her. Then Helen made it all a dozen times worse by saying cheerfully, 'Doesn't she look like an angel, Dr Patrick?'

Emma's face was instantly filled with colour. She gave Helen an exasperated look. But Patrick didn't laugh, and his eyes didn't waver. Only his voice was a little constrained when he answered simply, 'Yes'.

Despite the assiduous attentions of John Morrison at the party, Emma found herself watching for Patrick. It was stupid, she told herself. Ten to one if he did come it would only give her pain. For he was probably planning to go home and get Prudence. Emma knew it must hurt her, but she wanted to see the woman just the same.

In the event, though, he came without her. It was about nine o'clock. Emma had just about given him up when suddenly he was standing beside her, and her heart seemed to give a violent plunge. He looked wonderful. He'd changed his work clothes for casual trousers and a coat that fitted across his shoulders like a glove. All at once Emma didn't know what to say to him. He might have been afflicted in much the same way. They murmured a greeting awkwardly, like two strangers. Then, much as a stranger's might have done, his eyes lit on her glass. 'I'll get you a drink,' he said. 'What are you having?'

Emma in fact had decided not to have any more for now, but she quickly changed her mind. She needed a few moments to get used to the way he looked tonight. 'Scotch and soda,' she said, and he went to get her one. It would be her third, and she wasn't much in the habit of drinking. John Morrison had already brought her two before being trapped in conversation with Evan Thomas. She knew she'd better make it last. It didn't take many to make her sleepy.

He returned with two drinks, and Emma took hers awkwardly, beginning to sip it straight away for something to do. 'Do you remember anyone?' she asked him, since he stayed standing beside her, and he nodded.

'Quite a few.'

Emma wished in that case he would go and talk to them instead of looming silently at her side. She saw John Morrison detach himself from Evan and come their way. Shortly after he joined them, Patrick did excuse himself and go away.

The party was one of the least comfortable social occasions that Emma could remember. On the one hand, she had to work to stop herself from being monopolised by John. It wouldn't do any good to let him spend all his time with her. On the other hand, her eyes seemed to develop a will of their own, and constantly sought out the tall, handsome figure of Patrick as he chatted to those he knew. Somehow in a short time she found she'd finished her drink, and from the way she felt now she'd definitely had enough. Helen appeared then, with a friend called Martin whom Emma knew a little, and they fell into conversation. He was a radiologist with an inexhaustible fund of jokes, and was just what Emma needed. She relaxed perceptibly.

By eleven-thirty Emma had decided it wasn't such a terrible party after all. A few others had come to join them and the conversation was lively and amusing enough to take her mind off other things. Three drinks had done their magic, and she was feeling pleasantly expansive, her cares for the moment gone.

Soon, though, she began to feel tired, and decided she would go home. John had offered to drive her but she'd refused, preferring to take a cab and to keep him at arm's length. In any case, it was his party. He really shouldn't have offered to do it. She couldn't deny him the brief hug he always gave her. Tonight he followed it up with a kiss on the cheek. Emma left feeling she and John would soon need to have a talk.

In the foyer of the function-room, she went to the telephone, flipping the pages of the directory over to find the number of a cab. She jumped and almost dropped the receiver as Patrick's voice came from behind her.

'Are you calling a taxi?'

She turned round to face him. 'Yes. Do you want one, too?'

He shook his head. 'Car's outside.' He hesitated just a moment, then said, 'Come on. I'll give you a lift.'

Emma thought later that it was the alcohol that had robbed her of her caution and made her say yes.

'Where now?' he asked as Emma directed him.

'Left at the next,' she said, but then cried, 'No!' as he made the turn. Patrick pulled the car in to the kerb. 'Did I say left?' she asked guiltily.

She saw him grin suddenly. 'You did.'

'I meant right,' she confessed.

'How many drinks have you had?' he asked.

'Three,' she admitted.

He was still smiling. 'Not so many.' His eyes travelled over her. 'But you're only a small person,' he said.

Emma stuck her chin out. 'Are you implying I've had too much to drink? Let me tell you that I often say left when I mean right. I get it from my mother,' she declared.

He laughed and began to turn the car around.

It had broken the ice, and they chatted now as he drove the rest of the way. Emma began to feel more relaxed with him as they discussed the people who had been at the party.

'Evan's heart's in the right place,' Emma said. 'But if he corners you at a party the only way to escape is to shoot yourself.'

Patrick gave a hoot of laughter, and drew the car up outside the house that Emma had indicated. He switched off the ignition. 'Do many people do that?' he asked.

'Certainly,' said Emma, her mouth turning up. 'The floor's usually littered with corpses by midnight.'

Patrick laughed again. He leaned back in his seat and looked at her. 'What about that other chap—the deputy super?'

'Ross?' She raised her eyes to him meaningfully. 'Very *peculiar*,' she said with emphasis.

Patrick was smiling. 'Peculiar how?' he asked.

Emma shook her head. 'I don't think I can tell you.'

'Whisper it in my ear,' he grinned, sliding a little towards her.

Emma giggled. 'He stuffs things,' she whispered.

'All administrators stuff things,' Patrick said reasonably, and Emma gave a peal of laughter.

'No! Taxidermy. He has an office full of stuffed birds.'

Patrick gave her an arrested look. 'Feathered?' he said faintly.

Emma dissolved into laughter again. 'Of course feathered!' she exclaimed.

Patrick grinned down at her, the dancing light in his eyes visible even in the semi-dark. Emma's heart suddenly seemed to realise that she was sitting in a parked car inches away from him, and that he was laughing down into her face. It seemed to spurt into a different rhythm, one that throbbed at her throat.

Patrick himself had gone silent, until she heard him say in a hoarse tone of regret, 'Oh, God—what am I doing here? What a fool I am!' It was the utterance of a man who had come to his senses too late. Already he had reached out for her, and taken her face between his hands. As the words were said, he had turned up her face and covered her mouth with his own.

It paralysed her. The fierce, sweet touch of his lips seemed to dissolve her will. She let him kiss her. Then, as his arms went round her and drew her body against his, she began to kiss him back. This time she didn't think. She'd had just enough to drink to be careless of consequences, to feel that all that mattered was that Patrick wanted to kiss her, and that she wanted with all her soul to return his kiss.

Her free arm went round him as Emma let herself sink into his embrace. He removed his lips from hers and planted kisses instead upon her neck. Emma could feel his hot, quick breath there. It was a sensation too exquisite to resist. They clung together, Patrick still now, his arms enfolding her so tightly she could hardly breathe.

This time it was he who withdrew from her. He sat facing forwards, his arm on the back of the seat and his hand over his eyes. Emma's heart still pounded, but already she began to realise the foolishness of what they had done.

'Wonderful,' she heard him whisper in a voice with a bitter edge. 'You're tight and I'm stupid.'

'I'm not tight!' she said. 'I've had three drinks!'

'Yes,' he said. 'Would you have done that if you hadn't had any?'

Emma felt suddenly that she wanted to cry. 'I don't know,' was her miserable reply. Then, 'Why did you do it?' she flung.

Patrick dropped his hand and turned to look at her. 'It seems I can't help myself. Believe me—I had no such intention.' His voice was curt.

'Then why do it?' she insisted. 'I don't understand.'

'You think it's simple?' His voice was angry now.

'You're right. It ought to be. There's someone else. The feelings I have for you are way out of line. But I have them still, Emma. And you respond to me. Perhaps if you didn't I could get them under control. God knows I've tried. I don't want to want you.'

'Aren't you——?' Emma wanted to ask about his relationship with Prudence. Surely if he were happy there, he wouldn't have these feelings for her. She groped for a way to put it.

But he didn't give her time. 'Why in God's name do you kiss me back, Emma? Why can't you be cold?'

Was that what he wanted? For her to be strong enough for both of them, so that his illicit desire for her could be forgotten, and he could go on with Prudence as though it had never been? But how could he feel this way about her at all if he loved the other girl? It was alien to Emma. She wasn't made that way. 'Is it—possible to—have feelings for two people at once?' she asked miserably.

He looked at her, his face grim. 'Evidently it is,' he said.

Emma was silent.

'Oh, God, I didn't mean to do this to you,' he breathed. Abruptly he took her hand. 'Emma—is there no chance. . .?'

Emma pulled her hand away, tears of grief and anger coming to her eyes. How could he ask her to accept half-measure? How could he treat her like this—again? 'No!' she cried. 'I'm going in.'

Emma lay face down on her bed, crying in great rasping sobs. 'I hate him!' she wept, and for a moment felt that she really did. What did he expect her to do—to agree to see him secretly, to carry on an affair with him, while he went back to Prudence at the end of the day? Prudence—what a stupid name!

She could still hardly believe that this was Patrick Cavanagh, loving one woman and wanting another. Had she caused this change? Or had he always been like this, and she had been blind?

Emma rolled over and dried her face with a tissue. Then she wondered suddenly if he was trying to hurt her back. He knew she felt something for him. She had told him so. Was he out for revenge, his interest feigned? As Emma thought again of the way he'd kissed her, she knew that was wrong. He wasn't pretending. He'd kissed her with all he had. Patrick Cavanagh wasn't being sadistic. He was caught in a trap as surely as she. It was the trap of his own emotions. He was caught between his new love and his old. The real cruelty he had committed was in trying to have them both. That was cruel and selfish. She couldn't forgive him that.

CHAPTER EIGHT

EMMA woke feeling angry. She hadn't been at work long when she began to suspect that Patrick had done the same. It wasn't that he was rude or aggressive. There was just a certain brusqueness, and once or twice an impatience that was unusual in him.

He frowned at her once as he prepared to inject some cortisone into a patient's tennis elbow. She had drawn it up with a twenty-one gauge needle. 'That needle's too big,' he said.

Emma glanced up, surprised at the impatient tone. It annoyed her. 'I know that, Doctor,' she said. 'I'm only using it to draw up. There's a twenty-three there for you to use.' Her own tone, she realised belatedly, was crisp enough for the patient to glance at them with interest.

Patrick said nothing more, but there were several other occasions that day on which their usual cordiality seemed to desert them. Emma was aware that she was touchy. She tried to control it, but just the sight of his face seemed to hurt her and to bring back her anger at his selfish lack of principle.

'I'll do that,' she said as he started to re-dress a wound he had inspected. Dressings were a nursing job. She knew she could do it quicker and better herself. But she realised she had sounded snappish, and was not surprised when he glanced up with a cold look. He looked as though he would reply, but if he was going to snap back he bit back the words and only walked away.

It was inevitable perhaps that their sore spirits should draw them into open animosity. It was a pity it began in front of Mrs Cowley as they attended to her leg ulcer once again. She was a nice old lady, though she wouldn't keep her leg up, and she was fond of both of them.

'I don't think this type of dressing is helping,' Emma said. Since the choice of dressing was hers there seemed no sense in Patrick's becoming annoyed. But to Emma's ears he sounded it as he replied.

'I don't think the dressing has anything to do with it.'

Patrick had never contradicted her so flatly in front of a patient. Even where he plainly disagreed he'd been courteous enough to put his own point of view gently and politely. Emma felt an angry flush come to her face.

'What do *you* think it is, then?' she asked, sharply enough to make Mrs Cowley look at her in surprise.

Patrick clearly didn't like her tone. His eyes flicked up at her in an arctic glare. 'She hasn't been keeping her leg up,' he said bluntly.

It was probably true, but Emma no longer had the objectivity to consider his statement calmly. She only saw that he was ready to argue with her whatever she said, and that he had just been tactless with a patient who was fond of him. He might have realised it himself and been ashamed. A heightened colour had come to his face as he bent again over his work. Emma didn't notice it. Indignation had surged up in her and she had sprung to Mrs Cowley's defence. 'I'm sure Mrs Cowley has been doing as well as she can, Doctor. She has a husband to look after. Perhaps you hadn't considered that.'

Mrs Cowley looked at Emma's face and opened her

mouth as if to speak, but Dr Cavanagh had replied before she could.

'I'm perfectly aware of that, Sister,' he said with quiet venom. 'I don't need reminding of the social factors. The fact remains that this ulcer is not healing well.'

'I don't think that's the patient's fault,' Emma said, and saw an anger she had never before witnessed leap to his eyes.

'I don't think I said it was,' he replied through gritted teeth.

Mrs Cowley had been looking from one to the other as though she'd been watching a tennis match. In the seething silence that followed, she finally spoke. 'Oh, dear, dear,' she said in a tone one might use to children. ''Ave you two 'ad a spat?'

Patrick flushed to the roots of his hair. Emma's face, too, in seconds had turned a dull red.

'I'll tell you, love,' she said kindly to Emma, ''E *is* right. I've 'ad a lot to do lately. I 'aven't been keeping it up as much as I did last week. But I don't like to see you two quarrel. You usually get on so well.'

Emma felt they had both been reduced to the status of six-year-olds in the calm eyes of this amiable grand-mother. Patrick probably felt it too. He flung her a look over Mrs Cowley's head that plainly spoke a strong desire to murder her. They finished the consul-tation in silence. The only one to speak again was Mrs Cowley. 'Now you two bury the 'atchet, won't you?' she said as she waddled out of the door.

Had the patient not been slightly deaf, she wouldn't have been out of earshot before the storm broke.

'If you ever do that again, I'll strangle you!' Patrick's utterance confirmed what Emma had seen in his eyes.

'Do what?' she cried. 'You did it yourself!'

'Like hell!' he ground out. 'There's no justification for arguing in front of a patient!'

'Then I suggest you don't do it, Doctor!' she flung, and saw his eyes flame.

'It's the last time I do, Sister!' he said. 'Next time you're out on your ear!'

'Keep snapping at me the way you've done today, Doctor, and you won't have to ask me to leave!'

'Stop calling me that!' he shouted.

For some reason that she couldn't have named it made Emma want to laugh. It stopped her in her tracks. She faced him silently across the treatment-room, engaged in an inner struggle. It was too much for her. Try as she might to control her features, she felt her mouth turning up, and covered it at once with her hand. She shook. Patrick stared at her savagely. It seemed to make it worse. Emma gave up trying not to laugh. She took her hand away. With a shaking voice, she said, 'Wh-what a ridiculous thing to say!' Emma sat down on the treatment-room stool and laughed out loud.

When she looked up at Patrick again he had sunk into a seat and buried his face in his hands. She watched him for a moment. 'Are you laughing?' she asked.

'No,' he said hoarsely.

There was a silence. 'Why not?' she asked softly.

Patrick dropped his hands and gave her a look as bleak as his tone. 'Because I can't think of a single thing to laugh about.' He got to his feet and walked from the room.

'Oh, dear, oh, dear,' murmured Virginia as Emma told her about their troubles on Saturday. They were sitting once more in the 'nineteenth hole', the golf clubhouse, after finishing their round. 'How did it end?'

'I laughed,' said Emma.

'What?' chuckled her friend.

'Well, it was funny. We were like a couple of bickering eight-year-olds. We were calling each other "Sister" and "Doctor" in an offensive way, and he suddenly said, "Don't call me that!" It was ridiculous.'

Virginia grinned. 'Trust you to see the humour in it. Did he?'

'I hoped he would, but he didn't,' Emma said sadly.

Virginia was frowning now, swilling the drink round in her glass. 'Emma, I don't understand. This Prudence—can he really be in love with her if he still has these feelings for you?'

'I guess so,' said Emma. 'He more or less said it was a case of wanting two women at once.'

'I wonder if he's happy with her?'

Emma stared out over the green lawns. 'He hasn't said he's not, Ginny. He's not saying he loves me and wants to leave her. He just—is attracted to me still, and would like to have his cake and eat it, too.'

'You know, the way you've always spoken about him, I wouldn't have said he was the type for that. He's always sounded like a man who knew just what he wanted.'

Emma shook her head. 'Maybe I was wrong about him. Or maybe he's changed.'

Back at work on Monday, Emma reflected that their clinic was certainly proving a success. She looked at the appointments book and saw that most of the scheduled slots for the week were full. Patrick was perhaps more popular than Fiona, but only a little. In a few short weeks they had become a thriving practice, with patients who would now not go anywhere else. Evan

Thomas had asked them to provide ante-natal care for their regular patients to take the pressure off the hospital clinic across the road. In a short time they had a number of pregnant patients whom they saw on a Monday morning.

Emma went off to begin the list, performing her part before Patrick came to do his own. She weighed them, took their blood-pressure, tested urine and gave information, able to reassure them often that their experiences were normal and nothing to worry about. As she wrote her notes, Patrick would examine them and deal with any problems that had cropped up.

Emma had begun by feeling a little awkward after the débâcle of Friday afternoon. But Patrick behaved as though it hadn't happened. The only indication that anything was wrong was that he seemed to have reverted to the cold unresponsiveness he had shown at the start. In one way Emma was glad. It made it easier not to react to him. In another, it hurt her as much as it had at first.

'We'll arrange a scan for Theresa,' he told her, as the young mother put on her clothes. 'She's a little bigger than I expected her to be.'

'Could it be twins?' Emma asked, but he shook his head in a negative.

'No. Perhaps just a big baby,' he said.

Was he worried? Emma's eyes went automatically to his. But he only turned away. He no longer wanted to share his thoughts with her, nor any anxiety he might be feeling. Once more they worked like strangers through the day.

At least he didn't snap at her any more. But Emma began to find his chilling courtesy worse than his impatience had been. As forbidding as he was now, she could understand that Helen was a little afraid of him, and even feel disconcerted herself.

Perhaps that was why she forgot to mention the glucose in Mrs Grady's urine. She had meant to tell him straight away, but somehow it slipped her mind. It wasn't till he began to write his notes that she remembered it. And before she could open her mouth he'd seen it himself.

'What's this?' he asked, indicating her entry. 'Two plus glucose?'

'Yes. I'm sorry. I forgot to tell you,' she said guiltily, and saw his dark brows snap together in a frown.

'That's fairly important information, isn't it?' he demanded.

Emma felt the blood rush to her face. 'Yes,' she admitted. 'I'm sorry. I did remember, but only then.'

He continued to look at her, presenting a face as severe as he might have to any nurse who'd made a serious mistake. 'You're aware of the complications that can ensue if this patient has diabetes and we miss the diagnosis?'

'Yes,' said Emma a trifle breathlessly. Somehow today she wasn't tempted to argue at all.

'Then I think you'd better gather your thoughts a little.'

'Yes, Doctor,' she said automatically.

He didn't object to the title today. Nor did Emma have the slightest desire to laugh.

Over the next days, he continued to behave with cool formality. Emma was hardly able to believe that this was the same man who had kissed her so fervently in his car. He was totally different, except that he still looked the same. His face was just as handsome with its strong lines softened only by the beautiful passionate mouth. Even his eyes were cold, as they had been at first, though they still held as much alertness and intelligence as before. Her gaze sought him miserably at times, her feelings stirred by his face, or his strong, shapely hands or the muscular grace of his tall, athletic form.

Sometimes his eyes would catch her own, and then she would look away quickly, embarrassed and ashamed that she could still look at him like that. There was no answering warmth in him. He seemed to have decided to suppress any tenderness he felt, and to be succeeding very well.

'This may not be good news,' he said one day, handing Emma a piece of paper. It was Theresa Pettit's scan. 'She has polyhydramnios.'

Emma knew what it meant. There was too much fluid around the baby. It sometimes meant that something was wrong with the child. Emma knew a little sick feeling of dread. Theresa Pettit was so happy and proud about this baby. She was a nice girl, only twenty-two, with a sweet freckled face. Her husband was a factory hand, and they were poor. But Billy Pettit was learning a trade at night-school, determined to give his child a better start than his own.

Emma raised troubled eyes to Patrick Cavanagh. 'Did the scan show anything else?' she asked.

Patrick hesitated. 'Not really,' he said. 'The baby didn't move much during the scan. We'd better arrange for amniocentesis. It's best to know what's going on before the baby's born.'

Emma made the arrangements on the telephone. Theresa was nearing the end of her pregnancy. If something was wrong with the baby, there was nothing that could be done about it. But at least she'd have a few weeks to adjust. Emma had wanted to ask Patrick what he thought was wrong. A few weeks ago she would have. But now he was so uncommunicative, she let it go.

In any case John Morrison was once again propping up the bench in the staffroom. He'd taken to coming over several times a week in the lunch-hour. In one way she was glad to see him. He was always so pleasant and friendly. It made a welcome change from Patrick's behaviour. But in another way it troubled her. She hated the thought of having to tell him he was wasting his time. And she thought sometimes, like today, there was a specially hard look in Patrick's eyes when John was there. He didn't seem to approve of lunchtime socialising.

'Oh, no!' Emma groaned later that day and sat down without being bidden. Patrick had called her to his room to tell her the results of Theresa's amnio. He remained silent now, merely handing Emma the paper so that she could read of the diagnosis of Down's syndrome herself. 'But she's only twenty-two!' she said.

'It occurs in one in seven hundred pregnancies at that age,' Patrick said.

'It's awful,' said Emma, raising eyes full of hurt to him. For the moment she forgot the constraint that existed between them in her sorrow for her patient. 'Patrick—however will we tell them?'

A flicker of something showed in his eyes. But his voice was dispassionate as he said, 'I'll do that. They'll need a lot of support. They'll have to make a decision as to whether they want to care for the child themselves.'

Emma thought of the little jumpsuits Theresa had shown her. She had sewn them herself from cheap materials, and had decorated them with the shapes of rabbits and butterflies, sewn on by hand. Emma felt her eyes filling up. It was so unfair. She looked up to see what Patrick was feeling, but his eyes were on the report in his hand.

'I'll ask them to come in at the end of today,' he said finally, and Emma felt she had been dismissed. He didn't want to share the sorrow of it. She could only get up and go.

Emma couldn't help but be glad she'd been spared the worst when she joined the doctor with the Pettits at the end of the day. Patrick had called her in after telling them. Bill Pettit was leaning over a still sobbing Theresa, with a stricken look in his eyes. Emma knew that Patrick would have done this better than she could. Even now she felt a strong desire to cry. She a put a protective arm round Theresa's shoulder, and for a moment gripped Billy's hand.

'There's a decision you'll need to make,' said Patrick softly. 'Whether to look after the child yourself.'

Bill Pettit swallowed and looked at him. 'How—how bad will it be, Doc?' he asked.

'Right now, Bill, it's not possible to tell you. There's a range of intellect in people with Down's syndrome, just as there is in other people. Some of them function very well. Especially if they have the right care.'

'But—I mean—like, it won't be—a vegetable?'

Patrick shook his head. 'That's very unlikely, Bill. We have a patient here with Down's syndrome. Pete is twenty. He goes to work in a sheltered workshop every day. Catches the bus by himself. Shops for his mother on the way home. He's a very nice man.'

There was a silence. 'What does he look like, Doc?' asked Billy.

Patrick answered gently. 'Like a person with Down's syndrome, Bill. He has a wide, flat face. Slanting eyes. Sometimes he forgets to keep his tongue in his mouth.'

Theresa began to cry again.

Emma had been in some sad situations, but none seemed at the moment any worse than this. A dream had been shattered; the child the Pettits had hoped for was gone, with another different one in its place. Emma bid the couple goodbye at the door at last, and went to make herself a comforting cup of tea. Through the half-open door of the consulting-room, she could see Patrick, sitting at his desk still and staring straight ahead. 'Would you like some tea before you go, Patrick?' she asked.

He looked up abruptly, his thoughts interrupted. 'Mm—yes. Thanks,' he said.

As the kettle boiled, Emma's tears spilled over. She wiped them away, but several still glistened on her lashes when Patrick entered the room. He glanced at her face, then away again as he took his chair. She put his tea in front of him, then sat across from him to drink her own.

'It would have to happen to them, wouldn't it?' she sighed at last.

Patrick didn't answer for a moment, then said, 'Why not them?' in a voice she didn't recognise.

She looked up in surprise. 'They're so nice.'

Patrick's lip curled a little. 'So the misfortunes of this world should be reserved for those we don't like, should they?' His voice was mocking. 'Hardly calculated to make them any more likeable.'

Emma was silent. He was right, of course. It was illogical. But his hardness stung her anyway. Was the sympathy he'd shown the Pettits a sham?

'But—they've been working so hard to make a nice home for this baby. And they're such decent people. It makes you feel it's so unfair.'

'Why should it?' he said uncompromisingly.

In the silence that followed, for the first time Emma

truly wondered about him. Could it be that she'd been wrong about Patrick from the start? Could all his caring, all his gentleness have been nothing more ever than a clever façade? Could it be something that he turned on and off at will, just when it suited him? Emma sat arrested, her face in a heavy frown. Then the next thought followed logically: had he ever been what she'd thought in other respects? She'd known him two months when she'd become engaged to him. Was the fine character she'd seen in him a deception, too?

She shook her head as though to drive the thoughts off, and his eyes turned to her. They were stony.

'Don't like that thought?' he said. 'It doesn't suit your sentimental frame of mind.'

The sarcasm in it made her flinch. Why was he being like this? At a time when colleagues ought to support each other, it seemed he was being deliberately cruel.

'Don't you care?' she asked.

Patrick's voice was rougher than she had ever heard it. 'They don't need me to weep melodramatic tears over them. Nor do they need that from you. They need you to pull yourself together and offer them some practical support.'

Emma felt as though she'd been slapped. 'So—I'm not to feel anything?' she replied.

Patrick surveyed her coolly. 'Do you really feel anything?' he asked in a cynical tone. 'Or do you just imagine you do?'

Emma's lips parted in dismay. Did he really think that? 'No—yes! Of course I do!' she cried, her eyes wide. 'You must too.'

He shrugged one shoulder. 'It's a pity,' he said.

Emma stared at him open-mouthed. It seemed to fill him with contempt. He got up, tossing off the remains of his tea and setting the cup on the table with a clatter. 'In Africa healthy babies are born and their mothers watch them die of starvation. I don't see you crying about that.' Patrick gave her a hard stare from the door. 'Wake up to yourself, Sister.'

Tiger had taken to jumping up on the kitchen stool. He would sit there and watch her every move till his dinner was produced. The he would ignore her completely, his whole universe a plate of cat food. Emma opened the can absently, not even hearing his rasping request for her to hurry up.

She could only think about Patrick and wonder once again. Was he really the way he'd portrayed himself? If so, all his warmth and tenderness was assumed— assumed, she supposed, in order to be a good doctor— not something he felt in his heart at all.

If that were so, she didn't really know him. He might not have the principles with which she'd always imbued him. To cheat on a woman might be second nature to him. Or even to come here seeking revenge. Only one thing was certain—he'd just been callous enough with her to make her think long and hard.

CHAPTER NINE

'HELLO, John.' Emma found him in the staffroom again, propped against the bench and glancing through the morning paper as he waited for her. His good-natured face lit up in a smile.

'I just thought I'd pop over and tell you the blokes are coming tomorrow to put your fan in.'

'Oh, thanks! That was quick.' She looked at him mischievously. 'Is Cas shouting us the fan?'

John Morrison grinned. 'My lips are sealed.'

Emma was busy, but since he showed no inclination to leave she felt she ought to offer him a chair. He accepted happily and they spent ten minutes chatting. Emma found it a little awkward. She ought to be working now, not sitting around like this. When Patrick came to find her to give him a hand with something, she felt guilty and embarrassed.

'I'll get out of your way,' John said, and gave her his customary hug as he left her.

Patrick probably felt she should have been working too. Emma thought his face showed more than his usual disapproval. His forehead was creased in a frown.

She knew that he had seen the Pettits again. She had spoken briefly to them before they left. They were still shocked and grieving, still undecided about what they would do when the baby was born, but Theresa told her that talking to Patrick had helped. Emma had had an idea of her own about them, but she wanted to discuss it with Patrick before she mentioned it. An opportunity came at the end of their lunch-hour, when the others had left.

'Patrick, I had a thought about the Pettits.'

He looked up from the paper, his expression not really encouraging.

'Do you think it would help for them to meet Peter Walker?' He was their Down's syndrome patient.

Patrick frowned. 'With what in mind?' he asked.

Emma felt discouraged. She had thought it was obvious. 'So they can experience for themselves what a person with Down's syndrome is like.'

'Display him for them like a specimen?' His tone was cold.

Emma flushed. 'No!' she said indignantly. 'I think— if I explained it to Peter, he'd be only too willing to help.'

'And you think that would be a fair thing to ask him?' he said tartly.

'Why not?' she asked.

Patrick's mouth was grim. 'If you can't see that, I doubt if my explaining it would help.'

Emma flushed red again, but this time in anger. What an insulting thing to say! Several hasty retorts rose to her lips, but she managed to bite them back. But her voice shook a little as she said, 'I think that's very unfair. I don't think it would be exploiting Peter to ask him to do something which he himself would consider very worthwhile. He's intelligent enough to understand quite well if it's explained simply.'

Patrick regarded her hostilely across the table. 'And you think you'd be doing the Pettits a favour? Peter is a very special Down's patient. You know very well he functions much better than most of them. What if the child they end up with is only average, or worse?'

'I had thought of that,' she said. 'Have you asked

yourself why he functions so well? I know his mother.
I have no doubt that she has a lot to do with it. If all
Down's children were brought up the way Peter was,
maybe they'd all be able to do more. Shouldn't they
be shown the best that can be achieved?'

'Maybe they don't want that task.'

Emma spoke quietly. 'Maybe they don't. That's up
to them. But if I had to bet, I'd say they *will* keep the
baby. Wouldn't you?'

Patrick was silent, his eyes unfocused on the table.
In the end he shrugged a shoulder. He sounded bad-
tempered when he said, 'Do what you want.'

Emma thought about it carefully before she
approached the Pettits. Patrick's response had troubled
her. She had learned to rely on his judgement. She
reflected on it many times during the next week. But
when the day arrived for Theresa's next antenatal visit,
she still felt in her own mind that it would help.
Patrick's judgement in this case was warped, she felt,
by his resentful feelings towards her. Emma suspected
that nothing she suggested would find favour in his
eyes at the moment. He was not only cold towards
her, he was hostile.

Emma suggested it to Theresa almost casually. She
wanted to make it easy for her to refuse if that was
what she wished to do. Even believing it to be a good
idea, she was unprepared for the readiness of
Theresa's reply.

'Emma, could we do that?'

Emma nodded. She had already spoken to Peter.
He understood, and in his simple kindness wanted to
help. 'Would you like to?'

Theresa nodded in reply. 'I'd like to—only—I
wouldn't know what to say. Would he—understand
why I wanted to see him?'

'Yes. Peter understands that he's different from a lot of other people. He knows he has Down's syndrome, and that it makes some things hard for him. I've told him I have some patients who are going to have a baby with Down's syndrome and that they don't know much about it because they've never met anyone with it.'

Theresa had listened with close attention. 'Could Bill meet him too? I know he'd like to. I—sort of feel scared to meet him, Emma. But—if I don't, how will I know?'

Emma knew she should tell Patrick that she had arranged the meeting, but it was not something she looked forward to doing. She felt she could do without another dose of his hostility. In the event, however, he took it with no apparent emotion at all.

'When?' he asked, and when she had told him merely said crisply, 'I'll see them afterwards.'

Emma was glad. The meeting was sure to raise questions for them which only Patrick could answer. 'I—they do seem to want to meet him,' Emma said haltingly. She would feel so much better if Patrick agreed. 'And Peter understood exactly. He's a very generous person.'

But there was no unbending in Patrick. He offered her not the suggestion of a truce, but only received her words in stony silence.

It seemed best for the meeting to take place in the staffroom over a cup of tea. Emma warned the rest of the staff and seated the Pettits there, watching out for Peter in the waiting-room. He was calling by on his way home from work.

She knew he would be on time—you could always set your watch by him. At ten past four he bounced through the door. She'd never seen Peter looking anything but cheerful. Even when she'd had to give him a needle, he'd only said, 'Ouch!' and continued to smile. He was a short, stocky man with the wide, flat face termed 'mongoloid', but there was a light of infectious gaiety in his eyes. He spoke with only a slight impediment, his language simple. He was the friendliest soul on earth.

''Lo, Emma.' He had also to greet the receptionists before allowing himself to be led down the passage.

Emma had seen how nervous the Pettits were. There was little she could do to make it any easier. They got to their feet when Peter entered the room. Slowly and clearly, Emma made the introductions. Peter, smiling, put out his hand and shook theirs enthusiastically as he always did when he met someone new.

He hadn't got their names, though. 'What they called?' he demanded of Emma, and he repeated them after her, saying, ''Lo, Treesa. 'Lo, Bill.'

'Sit down, everyone,' said Emma, 'and I'll pour us all a cup of tea. OK, Pete?'

Peter nodded, smiling, then turned to Theresa and said with customary directness, 'You going to have a baby, Treesa?'

Theresa nodded her head. 'Yes, Pete. It's—the baby has Down's syndrome,' she said softly.

Peter nodded understanding. 'Like me,' he said.

'Yes,' Theresa answered, but clearly didn't know what to say after that.

It was seldom a problem round Peter Walker. He liked to talk and was never stuck for something to say. 'I got Down's syndrome,' he said cheerily. 'I'm slow.'

Emma handed them all a cup, and sat down beside him. 'What's it like, Pete?' she asked him gently to help them along.

Peter put his head on one side, and for the first time

she saw his smile fade as he thought. But then in a
moment it was back again as he answered, 'It's all
right. I can't count good. I work at the workshop.' He
thought some more. 'I can't play footie,' he said, then
an irrepressible twinkle came into his eye. 'It's all right.
I don't like footie.' Peter Walker laughed delightedly
as he always did when he'd made a joke.

Emma had never met anyone who could remain
immune to Peter's good humour. She glanced at the
Pettits and saw they'd both begun to smile. She'd also
never met anyone who didn't like him. This was a
simple man with a simple goodness. He was kind and
loving and it shone out of him for all to see.

'I make toys at the workshop,' he told them. 'For
children.' His voice was full of pride in what he did.

'That's lovely, Pete,' said Theresa. She'd begun to
look and sound more relaxed. Bill too was no longer
sitting so stiffly in his chair.

'Yeah. Trains. An' horses. Cars. Skipping ropes. I
can make toys for the baby,' he offered.

Bill Pettit looked touched. 'Thanks, mate,' he said
gruffly. 'That'd be real nice.'

Pete nodded, smiling across at them. 'Yeah. It's all
right,' he said. He paused for a moment as though
thinking again, then said simply, 'I'm happy.' No one
looking into that cheerful face could doubt it was true.

It was strangely moving. Emma felt tears prick at
her. She glanced at Theresa and saw her eyes had filled
up, too.

Peter Walker might be slow in many ways, but no
one could accuse him of being behindhand at picking
up on people's feelings. A little clumsily he reached
across the table. 'It's all right,' he said softly, and with
infinite gentleness stroked Theresa's hand. Emma had
never seen a gesture of comfort more effective. She

saw Theresa hesitate, then turn her hand over. Her fingers closed over Pete's, and he gripped hers in return.

Emma breathed a sigh of relief. It had gone as well as she'd hoped. Better, in fact. It was five o'clock now. For almost an hour they'd sat and talked. Pete had told them all about himself—where he lived, what he liked to do, who were his favourite friends. The conversation had moved from being slow and stilted to flowing easily with smiles and laughter. And most of it had been Peter's doing. He had the liveliest sense of humour and often surprised people with the wit of what he said. And it was Peter who had been intelligent enough to suggest that the Pettits talk to his mum.

When Emma ushered them into Patrick's consulting-room, the Pettits were looking calmer than they had since they'd known about it. Emma hadn't expected Patrick to want her there, but he glanced up and asked her to take a chair.

Theresa spoke before any of them. 'Thank you, Dr Cavanagh. For letting us meet him.'

He scanned her face for a moment, then said, 'It was Sister's idea.'

'Thanks, Emma. It's—it's made such a difference. I—had no idea. I guess I thought he'd be—some sort of monster. But—he's so kind!'

Patrick nodded. 'People with Down's syndrome seem to be particularly loving.'

'Yeah,' Bill chimed in. 'There's no bad in him at all. You can see it. He's a real nice bloke. I dunno about Terry. Well, we gotta talk about it. But I wouldn't mind having a kid like that at all.'

Theresa reached out and squeezed his hand. 'Neither would I,' she said.

Patrick was silent, pressing his fingertips together. 'It may not be easy,' he said quietly. 'Pete's probably like that because of the work put in by his parents.'

Theresa nodded. 'I know, Dr Cavanagh. I'm going to talk with his mum—so we know what to do.' She looked at him shyly. 'The thing is—me and Bill—we were thinking that we would probably decide to keep the baby anyway, whatever it was like. Because—because——' She groped for a way of putting it.

Bill explained it for her. 'It'd be ours,' he said. 'You can't just pretend it's got nothing to do with you and walk away. It's our baby. It's our responsibility.'

'Yes,' agreed Theresa. 'But it feels so much better now to know that if we work at it he might turn out like that.'

There was a moment of awkwardness when the Pettits had left. Emma had been so clearly right and Patrick so wrong that Emma was embarrassed. She wasn't the type to say 'I told you so', even when her antagonist had been rude and unpleasant. Accordingly she was prepared simply to say goodnight and leave him without speaking of it at all.

It was Patrick who did. But it was hardly an olive-branch that he offered her. 'That seems to have worked out,' he said, 'but don't delude yourself that it couldn't just as easily have been a disaster.' As he turned away to pack up his bag for a house call, Emma knew a childish desire to poke out her tongue.

She mastered it. With professional composure she merely said, 'I'll get you Mrs Ashleigh's file.'

Emma called Virginia when she arrived home, and they agreed to eat at an Indian restaurant just down the road. Informality was the key-note at the Taj. The owner and cook was an eccentric who expected patrons to set their own tables from a pile of crockery and cutlery on a bench. Raja didn't deign to wait on people. You picked up your plates of curry from the counter and carried them to your place yourself. The fact that there was no shortage of customers prepared to submit to this treatment bore eloquent testimony to the quality of his food. It was quite simply the best Indian food in the Southern hemisphere, as Virginia remarked as she sampled her Tandoori chicken.

It wasn't long before Emma had told her about the Pettits and Peter, and was pleased to find that Virginia at least heartily approved. She also told her friend of Patrick's behaviour, down to his parting words.

'Emma, the more you tell me about this man, the more he sounds like a complete pig. Are you sure you knew him before?'

Emma sighed. 'That's exactly what I've been asking myself,' she confessed.

Virginia enumerated his bad points. 'He's prepared to two-time his girlfriend, offers you an affair on the sly. He picks on you at work, is rude and insulting, and callous towards his patients.'

'Oh, no. He's not callous with the patients, Ginny. He's lovely with them actually.'

'To their faces,' Virginia answered. 'I've seen the type. They do it for their own image. They really couldn't care less.'

Emma was staring at the table, her curry growing cold. 'I don't know,' she said. 'I don't want to think that about him. He sounds as though he cares when he's with them. Up till the other day I would have said he sounded as though he cared when he wasn't with them too.'

'Until he realised he wasn't going to get what he wanted out of you.'

Emma flicked her eyes up at Virginia. She couldn't

deny it. It almost seemed to be true.

At work next day she couldn't help watching Patrick whenever they were together with a patient. The thought that she might have been deceived about him would not leave her mind. But his manner with the people they saw was as usual impeccable, whatever it might have been with her. He listened attentively, smiled, comforted, and gave every impression that their welfare and problems were as important to him as his own. Only with her was he unapproachable, his requests polite now, but his whole demeanour as cold and remote as the moon.

He only spoke to her about the patients. 'Mrs Ashleigh has a nasty laceration on her leg from that fall she had yesterday,' he said. She was the lady he'd gone to see after surgery. 'I've steristripped it for the time being, but I'd like to go back today and suture it. It will have to be at the end of the day.' He hesitated. 'I've no right to ask. . .'

Emma knew what he wanted. 'Of course I'll help,' she said.

'You haven't any pressing need to get away on time?' he enquired, and Emma thought there was just a tinge of sarcasm in it.

'Not at all,' she said crisply. 'What brought about the fall?'

There was a pause. Then, 'She's a little anaemic,' he told her. 'I think she hasn't been getting enough to eat.'

Emma looked up at him in surprise. It was not what she had expected to hear of Mrs Ashleigh. She was a rather unusual patient for the clinic—a well-spoken lady in her seventies who always came dressed in old-fashioned but excellent clothes—and Emma had wondered before why she would choose to visit a clinic designed for the poor. 'Why not?' she asked.

'The usual reason,' Patrick confirmed. 'Money.'

Emma looked at him, frowning. 'Is she poor?' she asked. 'She doesn't look it. Or sound it.'

'I think she wasn't once. But she is now. She's a widow. She was left with some savings and her house. But her husband died ten years ago. She's run through it. She still has the house, but no money. And she's sold all her furniture. Even her husband's war medals.'

'What?' said Emma. 'Doesn't she have any income?'

'No.'

'What about the pension?'

'She didn't think she was entitled to it. Because of the house.'

'Oh, no!' Emma groaned. 'That's awful. The poor old thing!'

'This fall's been very fortunate,' he said calmly. 'If I hadn't done a house call I imagine we would never have known.'

Emma felt appalled. To imagine a poor old lady all alone, selling off the things she'd collected and probably treasured, eking out the money by starving herself, and not knowing where she could turn at the end, brought a lump to Emma's throat. She might have said more once with a different Patrick, but now she controlled her dismay under his passionless eye.

'What can we do?' she asked, more of herself than him.

'I've explained to her that she is entitled to the pension. I rang Social Security this morning,' he informed her.

Emma nodded in approval. 'But her things . . . It's so sad,' she said. 'Does she mind about them very much?'

'I expect she does.' He gave his opinion in a dispassionate tone. 'But that's not our problem,' he said.

Emma's eyes flicked up to him. Once more her conversation with Virginia came to her mind. Could he
truly dismiss it like that? To Emma it seemed a tragedy.
Didn't he feel what the loss of Mrs Ashleigh's things
would mean? Emma watched him as he sorted through
the files for that of the next patient. His good-looking
face was unruffled, the strong features as equable as
ever. Emma had the feeling that the more she saw of
Patrick, the less she knew who he was or what he was
really like. She wondered then, in the face of that,
how her own feelings about him could remain
unchanged. For that was the other thing she discovered
during her scrutiny: she loved him as much ever.

Emma slid into the front seat of Patrick's car, and
placed the covered dish with the instruments in it on
her lap. He eased his tall frame into the driver's seat
and in a short time was guiding the car through the
traffic with capable hands.

'Social Security called back,' he told her. 'They're
prepared to issue a cheque in the morning so she can
buy some food.'

'Perhaps I can do some shopping for her,' Emma
suggested. 'It doesn't sound as though she's well
enough to go out.'

'She's not,' he said. 'But you'll find she's very proud.
She doesn't like to ask for help.'

Mrs Ashleigh's place was a neat Victorian house
with a lovely show of roses at the front. The front
door was reached via a shady veranda crowded with
pot-plants which looked a little neglected. Emma
guessed that Mrs Ashleigh hadn't been well enough to
do much gardening of late.

She answered the bell slowly. 'Oh, Doctor—come
in. How kind—Sister! How good you are! Oh, dear—

what a terrible nuisance I'm being.'

Both Patrick and Emma made sounds of reassurance as they followed her down the hall, but she continued to lament the trouble she was putting them to.
Emma's heart gave a little uneven lurch when they
reached the sitting-room and she saw the truth of
what Patrick had said. It was pathetically bare. Two
worn chairs were left and a cracked old table. Only
the marks on the carpet attested to where the old
lady's other things had stood. A few pictures were left
on the walls—things of no value to anyone else, Emma
guessed.

'Won't you sit down?' Mrs Ashleigh said. Emma
could see it was shame that had brought a tinge of
colour to the old lady's pale cheeks. 'I'm so sorry,' she
said in a crushed voice. 'I'm afraid there are only two
chairs.'

'No, thank you,' said Patrick. 'Sister and I have
come to work. If you'll be good enough to sit down,
we're going to patch up that leg.'

The laceration was quickly sutured. Emma had left
the other chair for Patrick to sit in while he did it, but
he silently pushed Emma into it and stitched up kneel-
ing on one knee on the floor. Emma cut the last stitch
at the length he liked, then Patrick rose, leaving her
to dress the wound.

'You must have a cup of tea,' Mrs Ashleigh said
when it was finished. She started to struggle to her
feet. 'It's all ready.'

Patrick had begun to decline politely when Emma
cut across him, 'That would be lovely, Mrs Ashleigh.
Very kind of you.' She darted a warning glance at
Patrick, and saw him quickly grasp her point. This old
lady had had her pride trampled on enough. They
couldn't refuse to accept a cup of tea. 'But I'll only

have one if I can pour it. Doctor wants you to keep your leg up.'

'Oh, yes, of course—how kind you are,' she rambled. 'It's all ready—just the jug—if you'll bring it to the boil again. I do like my tea nice and hot. Don't you, Doctor?'

Emma heard Patrick assent as she flicked the jug switch in the kitchen. Swiftly she took a look around. Even here was evidence of things sold to keep Mrs Ashleigh afloat. She glanced into the dining-room and saw that it was empty of the dining suite that had once obviously been there. What must it have cost the old lady to get rid of these things—probably for a pathetic sum—that she must have had for years?

Emma poured the water into the remaining cracked pot. There was tea in it already. While waiting for it to brew, she quietly opened the door of the fridge. There was little in it—a few rather old bottles of condiments, the remains of a loaf of sliced bread, a small carton of milk. She shut the door soundlessly and continued her search in the pantry cupboard. The story was much the same. As far as Emma could see the old lady had been living on bread and Vegemite. And, unless she was wrong, she'd just given them the last of her tea.

'If you can do without me for a while in the morning I'll go straight to Social Security and pick up her cheque. They'll cash it for her at the post office. I can do some shopping at lunchtime. She's got some bread and Vegemite, but nothing else.' Emma strove to keep her voice calm, but there was a painful knot in her throat.

Patrick nodded, his eyes on the road.

'I wish—I wish we could get her things back,' she

said in a muffled voice. 'I don't suppose she'll get enough pension money to buy them back.'

'No,' said Patrick.

'They wouldn't backdate it? Give her some back money?' she asked.

'No,' he said again. 'I enquired.'

'God, it's so sad!' Emma said, her voice cracking a little. 'Her husband's medals. Her rings. There must be something we can do!'

'There's no guarantee that they'd still be at the place where she pawned them,' he said unemotionally. 'Forget it. There's nothing to be done.'

Emma felt a sudden surge of anger at him. He really sounded as though it didn't matter at all. She wanted to shout at him—to tell him what she thought. He really didn't care. Angry words jostled one another in her mind. Virginia was right. It was all on the surface— just an effective façade. Underneath he was as hard as stone.

There wasn't any point in saying it, Emma suddenly thought. You couldn't get through to people like that. She gripped her seat and said nothing, his lips pressed together tightly. When they drew up back at the clinic, she bade him the briefest goodnight.

CHAPTER TEN

NEXT day in her lunch-hour Emma did Mrs Ashleigh's shopping. She had gone straight to her house in the morning with the cheque, and together they had worked out a list. The sight of Mrs Ashleigh's bare rooms had still made her unhappy and brought back the feelings of anger towards Patrick Cavanagh she'd had the evening before. Mrs Ashleigh had told Emma that he had promised to return this afternoon. Emma had to reflect that he took good care of his patients medically but it was the only positive thought she had about him just now.

The old lady's gratitude at seeing the things Emma had brought and her joy that the doctor had been right about the pension only seemed to make Emma sadder. If only they'd known a year ago, she wouldn't be living in this impoverished state now.

'You must miss your things,' she said gently, and was sorry she had as tears sprang to Mrs Ashleigh's eyes.

She fought them off bravely. 'Oh—I'm just so glad I can stay in the house. I thought I'd have to let it go. Charles and I lived here all our lives together. So many memories. . .' She trailed off mistily. 'Some things— were harder to part with than others,' she struggled to say at last.

Emma knew there was no point talking of getting them back. Mrs Ashleigh's pension wouldn't run to that. If she'd had any money herself, she would have gladly used it. Not for the first time, Emma berated herself for never having bothered to save.

When she returned to the clinic, she didn't feel like talking. Given Patrick's taciturnity, they spent a very quiet afternoon.

'Emma, Dr Patrick's taking tomorrow afternoon off,' Marje told her at closing time. 'Will that affect any of your patients? Do you want me to reschedule any?'

'Is he?' Emma glanced through her list. 'No—if any need to see him we'll have to get them back next week.'

'There'll be some time on Monday,' Marje advised. 'Tomorrow's going to be really busy. We were full already and we've had to put tomorrow afternoon's lot in too.'

'Great!' breathed Emma. Just when she was going out and had hoped to get away by a reasonable time. She shrugged. 'OK.' Paul Ryan would just have to wait. She wasn't so sure she ought have said yes to him anyway. He was a young surgeon. She'd known him for at least two years, but not very well. He'd chatted to her at the admin party and she'd decided she liked him. But she'd been surprised when he'd rung and asked her to go with him to another party on Friday night. She hadn't been conscious that she'd made an impression. She realised that she'd thought of little else than Patrick that night. It was in an effort to force herself to stop thinking about him that she'd said yes, she would go. As Virginia said, it was time she started seeing other men and trying to get Patrick out of her heart.

The only good thing about that Friday was the news that came in as they swallowed their morning tea. Theresa Pettit had gone into labour two weeks early. She'd had a boy at five that morning and both were well.

Fiona Whitely had been the first there and had taken the call. 'It was the husband who rang,' she said. 'Bill,

is it? He said it was as they'd expected. The baby
has Down's, but he's got no heart problems or other
abnormalities, and he's quite well.'

'Well, that's something,' said Anne. 'Poor
little thing.'

'Do you know—did he say how Theresa was
coping?' Emma asked.

'Yes. He said to tell you Theresa's fine. She's got
the baby rooming in with her.'

Emma breathed a sigh of relief. Sometimes it was
different when people came face to face with the
reality. But it sounded as though the Pettits hadn't
changed their minds.

The rest of the day was chaotic. They had far more
patients than they should have had. Emma worked as
efficiently as she could so she wouldn't be too late.
She kept working through the lunch-hour and was in
the treatment-room, tidying up after the previous
patient, when the others gathered in the staffroom to
eat their lunch. She cursed a little when she heard
John Morrison's voice in the staffroom asking whether
she was there.

'Yes, she's in the treatment-room, John,' she heard
Marje say. Fifteen minutes was wasted when John
came to find her for nothing more than a chat.

By four-thirty she began to think she was going to
be seriously late. She was bandaging a knee that
Patrick had just taken fluid from, and there were half
a dozen more patients to see. But Marje Gilbert had
come and given her news of a welcome respite.

'Sister Emma, Paul Ryan was just on the phone. He
says to say he's sorry, but he's going to be half an
hour late picking you up.'

Emma glanced up, flushing a little at having her
social life discussed in front of Patrick. But she only

said, 'Thank goodness for that. Thanks, Marje,' and went on bandaging the knee. The doctor, labelling the specimen, gave her the barest glance.

Emma scooted into the bathroom, stripped off in seconds and was under the shower by quarter to six. She felt she'd done well. It was a pity that hospital parties tended to start so early. But with the long hours that many of them worked, and the nights on call, people tended to fade out by the time midnight came.

She shampooed her hair quickly and turned off the taps. Pressing the water out of her hair with a towel first, she stood in front of the mirror to blow it dry. Finally she switched off the drier and combed out her abundant curls. She glanced at her watch on the shelf below the mirror—plenty of time. She could slow down. It hadn't occurred to her to slide the lock on the bathroom door. It was a hospital lock that registered 'engaged' and 'vacant'. When Patrick opened the door of the bathroom, Emma was poised stark naked before the mirror, putting her earrings in.

She flew round to face him, her mouth coming open in a little 'O' of surprise and dismay. Patrick had checked on the threshold, and stood as though rooted to the spot. His eyes travelled over her with the speed of light and arrived back at her face. He looked like a man struck.

It had only taken a second. Then he had backed out and closed the door. Emma, shocked and shaken, hadn't even reached for a towel.

Dressed now, and almost ready, Emma's hand still trembled as she packed up her things. If there was any consolation in the incident, it was that Patrick had looked as appalled as she had been. Emma mentally cursed herself for having been in too much of a hurry to have bothered locking the door. She had known he

was still in the building and that he had another patient
or two to see. She fervently hoped he had gone now as
she smoothed her dress nervously down over her hips.

It was another of those dresses that Helen would
have given a lot to have the legs to wear. Black and
form-hugging, like the other it came to just above the
knee. But it was more sophisticated in style. Virginia,
who had seen it once, had proclaimed it a knock-out.
The gold drop-earrings and a plain gold bangle were
the only ornaments Emma wore with it, but she didn't
need any other.

She picked up her bag and gingerly crossed the hall
to the staffroom, hoping to God Patrick wasn't still
there. It proved a vain hope. He was standing at the
sink with his back to her, scrubbing his nails. Emma's
heart lurched violently and broke into a cantering beat.
She glanced at the clock on the wall. Ten minutes till
Paul would be here. She thought all at once she would
sit in the waiting-room, but at that moment Patrick
turned round, drying his hands on a towel.

The merest hesitation in his movements betrayed a
reaction. His eyes met with hers a moment, scanned
the rest of her, then dropped to the task of drying his
hands. He hung up the towel, turning away from her
and, facing the window, spoke. 'I beg your pardon,'
he said formally. 'I didn't know you were there.'

Emma swallowed and answered him. 'Not at all. I
should have slid the bolt.' There was silence as Emma
decided she wanted a glass of water. Her throat felt
uncomfortably dry. She went to the cupboard and
reached up for a glass, hoping he'd move away from
the sink. When she looked around she found he had
turned towards her again, and was silently watching
her from where he stood. Stilling her disquiet, she
moved to the sink beside him. When she'd filled the

glass she glanced up again, and saw that he was leaning there, his arms folded, in his eyes a cynical glint.

She went to the table and perched on it, realising belatedly that it made her skirt ride up. His eyes raked her again, this time slowly, with what Emma thought was a kind of insolence. With difficulty she swallowed a mouthful of the water, wishing with all her heart that he would go away.

He didn't. Though she had looked away from him, she could feel his eyes still on her, and her heart still trotted along at an abnormal rate.

'Paul Ryan,' he said suddenly, and it surprised her into looking up. His voice was quiet, its tone vaguely mocking, like the expression on his face. 'I remember him. A good-natured, naïve sort of chap.' There was a pause, then he added, 'Like Morrison,' and there was no mistaking the sarcasm in his tone.

It was true. Emma herself had thought it. They were alike. But what was that to Patrick? And why was he saying it with a cutting edge to his voice and a hard glitter in his eyes?

'Is that what you like?' he asked, his tone frankly insulting.

Emma stared at him. What was wrong with him? Was he jealous of the other men that liked her? Was he, resenting the fact that she'd knocked him back, angry to see her going out with someone else? Damn him. What right did he have? All he had offered her were lies and cheating, a furtive affair that would end by tearing her apart.

'What's the matter with you?' she cried suddenly. 'Why are you talking like that?' She faced him across the narrow space of floor, her face flushed, her grey eyes sparking.

Patrick regarded her a long moment, his face twisted

by some inner pain. His voice when it came was harsh
and passionate, with an unexpected bitterness. 'I think
I'm going mad,' he said. 'I have no power to resist
you. It doesn't matter what I do.'

As Patrick moved, Emma slid off the table. She was
too slow to evade the man. She tried to side-step but
he shot out a hand and grabbed her wrist in an iron
grip. 'No!' he ground out, and jerked her to him. His
arms went round her in an embrace which ruled out
resistance. He looked down at her, his face taut, his
eyes dilated, then crushed her lips under his.

It wasn't a tender kiss that he gave her as he strained
her to his chest. It was a hard, harsh kiss that threatened to bruise her mouth. The arms that held her
weren't gentle or restrained. They gripped her with a
brute force that almost stopped her breath.

His mouth moved on hers, insistent and fierce. His
body declared its desire. She could feel the warmth of
him and the hardness, and his heart slamming in his
chest. She seemed to be drowning, fighting for air.
Shock and rage sprang up in her. But she hadn't the
strength to push him away. She had known he was
physically powerful, but she hadn't guessed the full
extent of it till today.

Emma began to feel frightened. She could feel he
was out of control. But it was also a fear of her own
reactions, for already she knew her anger was mingled
with desire. It was the single most arousing kiss she
had ever experienced, and passion flamed up in her
like a raging fire.

Perhaps he could feel it. Or perhaps he was beyond
the point where he cared. She felt his hands beneath
her buttocks, and he lifted her on to the table, forcing
her on to her back, his body pinning her full-length.
The thought leapt to her mind that he intended to

make love to her then and there. She had her hands free now and they came up to his shoulders, torn between the desire to caress him and to push him violently away.

But she had no chance to do either. He had seized her hands, and bore them down to the table over her head. He continued to kiss her relentlessly, his mouth fierce and urgent on her lips and her face and her neck. A gasp tore from her as he took both her wrists in one hand and brought the other one down to caress her breast. And through the white-hot heat of her arousal the anger surged up again.

How dared he do this to her? How dared he force her to feel what she had no wish to feel? A sob came from her, half choked by his possessing mouth. The tears welled up and spilled over, cascading over the sides of her face.

He raised his head and looked at her, his face the face of a stranger, taut with desire.

'Please!' she sobbed, but his face didn't soften. She thought his beautiful mouth had curled into a sneer.

'Please what?' he rasped in a tight, hoarse voice she hadn't heard before. 'I'm doing what you want.'

'No!' she cried. 'I don't!'

He kept looking at her, his face hard. Then slowly, deliberately he traced a line over her breast with his thumb. Fire shot up in her. 'I'm doing exactly what you want,' he said harshly. 'I see it in your face every day. Every bit of your body tells me so now. Shall I prove it?' He watched her face as his hand moved languorously, over her belly, down on to the inside of her thigh.

Panic engulfed her. She shook with a sob. 'No!' she almost screamed. 'I hate you! Let me go!' She began to struggle, her teeth clenched, rage flashing out of her eyes. She saw his face change, and in a moment he had done as she'd asked. She wrenched herself off the table and stood for a second, fighting for breath as he faced her silently. Then she launched herself forward and dealt him a ringing slap.

It was hard enough to knock a less powerful man off balance. It only jerked his head back and made him wince. Emma saw the blood come immediately to her hand mark. But he didn't move, and didn't say a word.

Emma struggled to control herself. She wanted to do it again. 'I hate you!' she flung at him instead. 'You're a fake and a cheat and a bully! If I never saw you again, it'd be too soon!' Her voice dropped to a low, grating rasp. 'I'd make love with anyone before you.'

Only now she saw him react. His eyes were flooded with unmistakable pain. He didn't stay for any more. Patrick turned on his heel and left the room.

Emma cried quietly as she washed her face in the bathroom, and applied her make-up again. Just minutes after he had left she heard Paul Ryan calling to her, and called back that she wouldn't be long. She had never felt less like going to a party in her life.

She couldn't have said afterwards that she had enjoyed it. She had chatted, danced and laughed, but it was with a hollow feeling in her heart. Paul Ryan was pleasant and fun but she had only really wanted to get away by herself and lick her wounds.

Tiger was waiting for her when Paul dropped her off. He complained trenchantly about the erratic nature of the service, but said he'd overlook it this once when she slung the bowl of cat food on the floor. She sat in the kitchen waiting for him to finish it so that she could kick him out again. Patrick's face kept coming to her mind.

What had made him behave so terribly? Your face tells me you want me every day, he'd said, or some such thing. Could it be true? Patrick had been hiding his emotions quite well. She had begun to think he had come to dislike her, that his attraction had died. She knew now it hadn't. There was no mistaking the force of the sexual passion that had burned in him. And there was no doubt in Emma's mind that what he wanted from her was sex.

She wearily mounted the stairs to her bedroom. OK, she admitted to herself, she had also hoped at first that there was something of love. She didn't think so now, not after that piece of mocking savagery.

She left her clothes on the floor where she had dropped them and crawled into bed. The trouble was she still burned with the memory of his touch. She drove out those feelings by thinking that every ill thing she'd ever thought of him was true. He was harsh, cruel and unprincipled. She would be angry with him for the rest of her life. It was a long time before Emma fell asleep, and then it was with fresh tears upon her face.

CHAPTER ELEVEN

EMMA stopped on her way to work on Monday and
sent flowers to the hospital for Theresa Pettit. When
she arrived at the clinic, Anne had a further bulletin.
They had decided to call the baby Patrick after Dr
Cavanagh. Emma's lip curled. If they had heard him
speak so callously of them that day in the staffroom,
she was sure they wouldn't have done it. Perhaps
they wouldn't have done it if they'd seen him on
Friday night.

She said nothing, but only checked through the
appointments book. She wanted to visit Mrs Ashleigh
this afternoon on her way home, but she wouldn't do
so if Patrick was going. There was no visit down for
him. Emma decided to skip their morning cup of tea.
She didn't want to see him before she had to. In the
event she didn't clap eyes on him till just before lunch,
when he buzzed her to help him with a procedure. She
had the impression he wouldn't have asked for her
help if there was any way he could have avoided it.
She thought she had never seen him look so drawn.

They completed the task in absolute silence. Emma
made a move to slip away without a word at the end.

But he prevented her. 'Stay a moment, please,
Sister,' he said. She thought his voice was strained.
He finished his instructions to the patient as Emma
stood debating whether she would ignore him and
leave. Then, the woman gone, he turned to her. 'I
want you to know I've decided to leave here,' he said.
There was silence as they faced one another. His face

144

was gaunt, a look of suffering in his eyes.

A spasm of pain seized Emma's heart, but it was rapidly followed by anger. So what did he want her to say? 'Good,' she said flatly. She saw him flinch as though it had hurt him. Illogically, it made her more angry than before. 'What did you think I'd say?' she flung at him.

'Just that,' he said softly. 'It's what I deserve.' He turned away, seemingly to gaze out of the window. Emma was conscious of a desire to wound him as he had wounded her.

'Don't tell me you're sorry,' she said savagely. 'You told me that once before. It's only a ploy to escape the consequences of your actions. One more fraud like the fraud you practise on your patients—on us all.'

He had swung around again, a look of dull surprise in his face. Emma continued, 'Don't think you fool me any more. I know you don't really give a damn about any of them. You don't feel anything for them. You just pretend. You don't feel anything for me apart from lust. You couldn't care less about me as a person. I don't suppose you feel anything about——' She was going to say Prudence, but found she couldn't say the name. 'About anyone,' she finished.

He hadn't taken his eyes off her during the speech. He seemed to sink now into his chair, and ran his hand over his face. She saw it was trembling. So, he didn't like to hear the truth about himself. His voice when it came was a whisper. 'I can't answer you,' he said. 'Not now.'

Emma cried once more in the bathroom, this time remembering to lock the door. He didn't matter, she told herself. He wasn't the man she had thought him anyway. He wasn't the sort of man she could love. It

made her wonder why she felt such anguish to think
he would be going away again.

In the afternoon they had a visit from Peter Walker.
It was a bright spot in an awful day. He wanted to tell
them all about the baby. Bill had picked him up and
taken him to the hospital in his car. He had seen Terry,
as he called her now, and she had let him hold
the child.

Emma took him into the staffroom, so that he could
sit and talk to them there. She could see that something
very significant had happened to Peter Walker.

'Hello, Doc,' he said to Patrick, who was talking to
Fiona. 'Hello, Doc Fiona.' It tumbled out before he
could take a breath. 'I saw the baby!'

'Theresa's baby?' asked Fiona. She knew all about
his meeting with the Pettits.

'Yeah,' he said, 'Terry's baby.' Peter was grinning
from ear to ear. 'Emma—I got this.' He rummaged
in the bag he always carried, and brought out an item
in a department-store bag. With infinite care he
unwrapped it. It was the sweetest possible teddy bear.
He looked up at Emma a little anxiously. 'Is that all
right, Emma?' he asked.

Emma smiled, her heart warmed. 'It's beautiful,
Peter. It's just right.'

His face relaxed into a beam. 'It's a little bear,' he
said. 'It's a little baby.' He laughed.

'It's lovely, Peter,' chimed in Fiona. 'It's just the
right size for a baby.'

'Yeah.' He nodded. 'I'm gonna make him lotsa
things,' he said. 'Not now. Too little now.' Peter had
wrapped the bear up again and put it away. He held
out his hands to show them how big Terry's baby was.
'This big,' he said.

Emma nodded. She was curious about something.

'Did you buy the bear yourself, Peter?' she asked.

'Yeah,' he said proudly. 'I bought it. I got money in the bank. I bought it. Grace Brothers.'

'Have you ever shopped at Grace Brothers by yourself before?'

'No,' he said, then smiled. 'It's all right. The lady helped me.'

Emma began to think this baby might be going to do something for Peter, and in fact that it already had.

'So what do you think of the baby, Peter?' It was Patrick who asked.

Peter's beaming face gave them the answer before his halting words could. 'He's beautiful,' he said. 'I love Terry's baby. He's my baby, too.'

When he was gone, Fiona was the first to say anything. 'Gosh,' she said. 'That choked me up. How wonderful for him.'

'Imagine him going to buy that bear,' Emma said softly. 'You know, this could be really good for him. He'll never have a baby of his own.'

There was silence for a moment, broken by Patrick. 'I hope it will be good for him,' he said. There was a grimness about his tone.

It sounded critical to Emma. She rounded on him. 'I take it you don't think so,' she said crisply, her eyes issuing a challenge.'

Patrick met her gaze with a sober gaze. 'It's not his baby—it's Theresa's and Bill's. It's possible he may get too involved.'

'You think the rest of us are stupid, don't you?' she demanded. 'You think we haven't considered that, and talked about it before Bill took him to see it?'

'Not stupid,' he snapped, looking stung. 'Just carried away with maudlin sentimentality.'

Emma swelled with rage. For a moment she couldn't

answer. Then, 'You would think so,' she said.

Patrick didn't answer, but only left the room. Fiona Whitely stayed where she was, her mouth half-open in surprise. 'I didn't know you two got on so well,' she said ironically at last.

Emma gave her a pained look. 'We don't get on at all,' she said, suddenly seeing that she could turn this to advantage.

Fiona studied her. 'I thought you worked together in Cas. Why didn't you work with me and Helen with him?'

'We did,' answered Emma. 'I—Helen didn't really want to work with him. And—I thought we could get over our—antipathy.' Emma began to find Fiona's silent gaze disconcerting. She continued briskly. 'But we haven't got over it. Fiona, would you mind if I worked with you?'

'Of course not,' she said. 'Will Helen agree?'

'I'm prepared to beg,' said Emma.

But she didn't have to beg at all. Helen had recovered from the worst of her nervousness of Patrick. She agreed readily enough when Emma explained that she and Patrick had been having major disagreements.

'That's funny,' Helen remarked. 'I thought he really liked you.'

'Well, he doesn't,' Emma said firmly. 'And I don't like him.'

Emma found an opportunity to tell him just before the end of the day. He looked up quickly from his notes, and regarded her with a grim look on his face. But he didn't argue. He just said, 'Very well. You'll only have to put up with the situation for a month anyway. My resignation takes effect then.'

She knew he had been to the hospital in the lunch-hour. He must have gone to Admin to resign from the job. A mixture of feelings assailed her—relief, satisfaction, grief and a terrible feeling she couldn't name that might have been the beginnings of a profound emptiness. 'I'm sorry,' she found herself saying. 'You—liked this job. I would have left if you'd wanted.'

It seemed to make him angry. 'I've told you my feelings about that. I don't want to hear you say you're sorry again. Spare me that.'

Emma looked at him uncertainly. She didn't quite understand.

He was continuing, 'In any case, I don't want to stay here. It was a mistake coming back again. I wish I'd never done it.' Emma could hear from his voice that it was true.

'What will you do?' she asked softly.

He shrugged. 'Return to Britain. Perhaps—I don't know. It doesn't matter.'

Emma wondered if his girlfriend would like that. 'The patients will miss you,' she said.

Patrick looked at her ironically. 'Will they?' He didn't sound as though he believed it.

For the first time she felt really sad for, him. People who didn't have real feelings for others, whose warmth was only an act, must miss out on such a lot. 'You don't understand,' she said softly. 'They really love you.'

'I don't care whether they do or not,' he said roughly. 'What does it matter?'

Emma knew it was useless. She gave up and went away.

'Bye, love,' Marje called, and Emma waved a hand. She had almost decided not to see Mrs Ashleigh today. But the thought of going straight home to no better company than Tiger didn't attract her either, so she let her bus go past and boarded the one that would take her to the old lady's place instead.

It was a short walk from the stop. At the door she paused a moment, composing herself, knowing that her spirits were raw already. She didn't need to feel any more sorrow today. In any case, she was here to help Mrs Ashleigh, not to grieve over her plight. It helped that Mrs Ashleigh herself was smiling when she opened the door.

'I saw you through the window,' she said. 'So kind of you to come and see me. Come in, my dear. So kind of you all.'

Emma stepped into the hallway.

'Would you like to put your bag here?' Mrs Ashleigh asked. 'I'll make you some tea. I feel so much better— I can't tell you.' She put her thin hand on Emma's arm and gave it a squeeze, looking up smilingly. 'I'll make the tea today.'

Emma smiled back. How nice to see her looking so much happier. Then they stepped into the sitting-room, and Emma gave a gasp. Part of her mind had noticed but not grasped the import of the chest on which she had been invited to place her bag in the hall. Now she realised—it had not been there before. And neither had any of things which now met Emma's astonished gaze. Mrs Ashleigh gave a delighted crow beside her as Emma stared open-mouthed around the room. It was fully furnished, in rather beautiful pieces of a period gone by. There was a Chippendale sofa in a Sanderson print, two matching chairs, polished pie-crust tables, an oak roll-top desk and much more. Even the pictures had been returned to the walls.

'Mrs Ashleigh!' breathed Emma, and the lady squeezed her arm.

'Yes, yes!' she cried excitedly. 'Come and see, my

dear!' The old lady led her from room to room. Emma could see that all was exactly as it must have been before.

'It's wonderful!' Emma cried. 'I'm so glad!' She turned to her patient and gave her a hug. Constance Ashleigh hugged her back, smiling up at her with shining eyes.

'Everything! He found everything!' she said, her voice cracking as her eyes filled with glad tears. She fished in her sleeve and dabbed at her eyes with a hanky. 'However shall I thank him?' she asked. 'So very, wonderfully kind!'

'Who? Who found it all?' asked Emma. She hadn't known the old lady had anyone alive.

'Dr Patrick!' she said joyfully, and Emma stood stock-still as though turned all at once to stone. But Constance was bubbling with happiness. 'I had no idea,' she said. 'Of course, when he came to see me he told me that those nice people—Social Security, I know they're called—he said they would give me some back-pay, he called it. He asked me for a list of all the things I'd sold and where I'd sold them, because he said I might be able to afford to get them back. I didn't think—well, I thought they would already be gone, and some of them were, I think, but he wouldn't tell me—he must have gone to so much trouble. Oh, dear, am I making any sense at all?'

Emma nodded dumbly.

'Sit down, my dear, and I'll try and gather my wits together.'

Emma needed badly to sit down. Woodenly, she sank into a chair. At the end of ten minutes she had it tolerably straight. Patrick had obtained a list of her cherished belongings, had hunted them down all over Sydney and had bought them back with his own money.

That Constance didn't know. But Emma knew enough to be sure of it. It made her want to laugh that Constance was almost inclined to give the people at Social Security equal credit in the recovery of her treasures. Nothing else about the situation made her want to laugh at all. She thought of Patrick. She had cruelly and miserably misjudged him. Unless—had her speech moved him to this?

'When did Dr Cavanagh tell you he thought you could get your things back?' she asked.

'The very first day, when he came to see me,' Mrs Ashleigh replied. 'He bathed my leg and put those sticky things on. I told him—all about everything. It seemed so easy to talk to him. Then he wrote a list of all the things. I didn't think it was possible then. I thought—well, you know—he could see how much I cared. I knew he wanted to help me, but,' she finished with a glow of gratitude, 'I didn't dream he would succeed.'

Emma found she couldn't bear to think of it any more just now. But it wasn't easy to get Mrs Ashleigh off the subject of Dr Cavanagh. Emma was forced to listen to a paean of praise. She was glad when the old lady's attention turned to her husband's medals, ranged on the mantelshelf, and they could talk of Charles Ashleigh for a space. They drank a cup of tea together, poured from a dear little Royal Albert teapot, placed on one of the pie-crust tables. Emma could see how much Constance loved these things, and it made her want to cry.

She got away at last after having a look at the leg. The wound was healing quickly and her patient stronger already, now that her nutrition had improved. It wouldn't be long, with the doctor's iron tablets, before she was back to her old self.

*　　　*　　　*

'You're joking,' said Virginia. She had come round in answer to Emma's urgent summons as Emma had known she would.

'I am not,' Emma said, sitting across from her at the kitchen table.

Virginia looked over to where Tiger was clawing at the enamel of the refrigerator and said absently, 'Do you think you should feed that cat?'

Emma burst into giggles. 'Damn the cat!' she said. Her face became serious again. 'Ginny, what does it mean?'

Virginia ran her hands through her hair. 'It wasn't what you said to him that made him do it.'

'You weren't listening!' cried Emma. 'He took a list of her things and where she'd disposed of them the first afternoon. Long before I spoke to him.'

'He had compassion for an old lady, then. He wanted to help her. He did.'

'Then why did he sound as though he couldn't have cared less when I was talking to him about it? Why didn't he tell me what he was intending to do?'

'Logically, he didn't want you to know.' Virginia looked at her. 'Did he expect you to go and see this old bird again?' she demanded.

Emma shook her head. 'I went off my own bat. Just—because I felt sorry for her. I wanted to see how she was.'

'Then we must assume he didn't want you to know.'

'Like he didn't want her to know he'd used his own money,' Emma said.

'You didn't tell her?' Ginny asked.

'No, of course not. He was right to tell her a lie about that. I think she'd be terribly troubled to think he'd done that.'

Virginia shook her head. 'None of it makes sense.

Will the real Patrick Cavanagh please stand up?'

'That's how I feel. He's unfaithful to the woman he's living with—or he's prepared to be—he's a monster to me, he's rude and aggressive towards me when I've knocked him back, he sounds as though he hasn't any sympathy for the patients, and then—he does that.'

'"He sounds as though he hasn't any sympathy for the patients",' Ginny repeated slowly. 'He sounded as though he didn't care about Mrs What's-her-name. Emma, it strikes me that you can't place too much dependence on the way this man sounds. That is not the action of someone who feels nothing for people, who doesn't care.'

Emma stared at her. 'So why did he talk like that?'

Virginia spoke quietly. 'Do you think this is a man who is so angry with you that when he speaks to you he can't sound any other way than harsh?'

'Yes. It could be,' she whispered. 'So, why?'

'Old wounds,' suggested Virginia. 'Maybe he's never forgiven you.'

'Yes, of course. That's logical. But——' Emma's face was creased in a frown '—it can't be that simple. He—was quite nice for a while. Till—till I knocked him back.'

'So maybe he loves you still.'

'Don't put that into my head, Ginny. He's living with someone. I was prepared to believe that he cared to some extent, even that he was torn between the two of us. But if he really loved me, if he cared enough to be hurt and angry still, he'd leave his girlfriend. Wouldn't he? How could he be happy with her and stay with her if he really loves me?'

'I don't know, Em. Maybe it's not that simple. I just don't know.'

At the end of a long night of reflection, Emma

decided that neither did she. Maybe it was an aberration. He was different with little old ladies. He had a soft spot for them—they reminded him of his mum. He hadn't been very sympathetic towards the Pettits. Maybe you had to be over seventy-five.

CHAPTER TWELVE

EMMA began work with Fiona the very next day. It was a relief for her only to see Patrick at their breaks. She thought he looked more relaxed too as the week went on, though she couldn't have said he looked happy. Well, it was not to be expected. It couldn't be pleasant to have come twelve thousand miles to do a job that interested you, then have to abandon it and go back. At times Emma found herself feeling guilty, until she mentally shook herself and reminded herself that it was his fault more than hers.

She still thought about the night of the party. Every now and then would come unbidden to her mind the memory of that savage embrace and the terrible magic of his touch. They had not made love when they were together before. Emma had wanted to wait. Perhaps she had been a little nervous, a little afraid she would disappoint him. He was a man of experience. Patrick had seemed to understand it without it being said, and hadn't pushed. He had held her and kissed her, and she had known how much he wanted her, but he had held himself under tight control.

There had been none of that on that evening in the staffroom, and little gentleness about him. Anger flared up in her still each time she thought about it. He had behaved terribly towards her. The only thing to be said in his favour was that he realised it himself and knew he had to go away. Emma thought back to their conversation afterwards when she had refused to accept his apology. She thought she had probably been unjust. He had been sorry. Even now, on the rare occasions when his eyes came to rest on her, there was sorrow in them, as though he couldn't see her without regret. After that last disagreement about Peter Walker they hadn't clashed again. He had reverted to being polite and quiet, his good-looking face once more dispassionate. Emma herself determined to be calm and courteous. It was only when those memories assailed her that a disturbing mixture of anger and desire awoke in her. At times she couldn't stop herself from wondering what it would be like to make love with Patrick. She would never know.

She still didn't know what to think about his actions with Mrs Ashleigh, and the hard words he had said about the Pettits. Was he capriciously kind—just when it suited him? Or had that harshness really been directed at her? Emma had finally to remind herself that it didn't really matter what he was. In a few short weeks, he would be nothing but a memory. He'd be gone from her life for good.

On the next Monday afternoon, the clinic enrolled a brand-new patient. Terry and Bill Pettit brought in the baby to be checked and weighed. It was Helen's job now since the Pettits were Patrick's patients, but Patrick called Emma in.

'Patrick wants you,' Fiona told her, and she went to the treatment-room in a little surprise.

Emma's heart gave a thump as Patrick looked down at her. 'I thought you might like to see this little citizen,' he said.

She quickly turned away from him and saw that Theresa Pettit stood with a bundle in her arms. Patrick's namesake was quite a big baby, with a great deal of dark hair. His face was the round, flat face of the Down's child, the eyes wide-set and a slanting almond shape. He was awake but quiet, placidly surveying the world.

'He's such a good baby,' said Theresa. 'He never cries. Mrs Walker says Peter didn't either. She's such a nice woman, Emma. She wants to help us. She's offered to baby-sit Patrick whenever we want to go out.'

'Wonderful!' Emma said. 'Take advantage of it!'

Theresa laughed. 'Don't worry, we will. I think she really wants to. She only had Peter. She says she hasn't enough to do.'

Emma smiled. 'Then you'll be doing her a favour. And you couldn't have anyone better to look after him, could you?'

'Pete said he'd call in here on his way home from work,' Bill Pettit told them. 'He wants to know what the baby weighs now. He knows by heart what he weighed at birth and how long he was and everything.' Bill grinned. 'He thinks this little bloke is the best thing since sliced bread.'

Emma laughed. 'We noticed that,' she told them. She suddenly thought of what Patrick had said. 'Has he—is he getting under your feet?'

'No!' Bill and Terry said together. Terry continued, 'He's great! He's the world's most considerate person. Bill had to twist his arm to get him to the hospital, even though he was dying to come. No. He'll never be a nuisance.'

'Terry gave him Patrick to hold in the hospital,' Bill said, 'and he was that pleased, he just looked and looked at him. And I thought, Gee, I hope we're doing the right thing. Like you said, Emma, I thought, What if he gets too involved? Then after a while Patrick was getting hungry, and he started to cry. Pete made the funniest face. He got up and handed him to Terry with a big grin. He said, "Here's your baby, Terry." I thought, No—there's no problem. He's a normal twenty-year-old bloke.'

They all laughed. Emma could picture him doing it.

'Here's Peter now!' announced Helen.

He came in with his customary grin and greeted them all by name before he went to look at the baby. 'What's he weigh, Terry?' he asked. Terry told him and he thought, concentrating hard and repeating what she had said. Finally his face relaxed into a grin again. 'He's bigger,' he said.

'Yes.' Terry laughed. 'He's six ounces bigger.'

'Six ounces.' Peter beamed. 'He's a good boy.'

It was terribly touching to see the interest Peter took in him. Patrick had to show him the tape with which they had measured the baby's length and indicate where he came to. Theresa passed the baby to Peter and he held him with all the tender care one might have lavished on a priceless treasure. He beamed all the while.

'I think you're going to make a very good uncle, Peter,' Patrick remarked.

He couldn't have said anything that would please Peter more. He looked up at the doctor, wide-eyed at the new thought. Then his grin stretched ear to ear. 'Yeah!' he said. 'I'm an uncle! Uncle Peter!' He appeared to find it very funny. He laughed delightedly.

Emma felt a contraction at her heart as she watched the little group—Bill Pettit grinning and saying, 'Uncle Pete,' and clapping him on the shoulder; Terry's sweet freckled face, relaxed and smiling, accepting the fact of this different child; and the joy of the kind, oddly made man who saw his own face reflected in that of the baby.

'Yeah,' Peter said softly, talking to the baby. 'I can't have a baby. I got Down's. But I can be an uncle.'

A lump had come to Emma's throat. Tears pricked at the backs of her eyes and one ran suddenly on to her cheek. She brushed it away with one finger and quickly looked around to see if anyone had noticed. Patrick was standing back against the wall, his head bowed. Perhaps he felt her gaze on him, for he glanced up for a second. That was all the time it took for Emma to see what no one had been meant to. Patrick's own hazel eyes were decidedly moist as well.

It was a long time before Emma could stop thinking about it, and about what he said later. For she passed him in the hallway after the Pettits and Pete had gone, and he hesitated and stopped.

'You were right. I'm glad,' was all he said, but Emma couldn't mistake the sincerity in it. She attended the next few patients with only half a mind as she tried to come to terms with the riddle that was Patrick Cavanagh.

She could only conclude that as far as his attitude towards his patients was concerned she had been completely and utterly wrong. He cared as much as she did. If he had spoken harshly it was because of her, and nothing to do with the patients at all. He was attracted to her still against his will. And she had rejected him a second time. The anger and hatred of fourteen months hadn't left him, even the love of another woman unable to drive either emotion from his heart.

It was beginning to be hot. At lunchtime next day Emma escaped into the back garden and sat in the shade with her feet up. Patrick came out, obviously with the same idea, and checked when he saw her. He looked as though he would have liked to go away again, but it was too awkward. Slowly he came forward and stood by the garden bench.

'Do you mind if I sit here?' he asked.

Emma shook her head, and prepared to move a little, dropping her feet.

'Don't move,' he said in a low voice. 'I didn't mean to disturb you.'

In a way Emma was glad he had come. She had spent most of last night thinking about him, and had come to the conclusion that she owed him an apology. In many ways his behaviour had been bad, but there were some things she'd said that just weren't true. Her face burned as she thought of the way she had called him a fraud. She screwed up her courage and spoke. 'I want to apologise, Patrick,' she said, before her resolution could fail her.

There was a little pause during which Emma didn't dare to look at his face. If she had she would have seen the signs of surprise. She continued, 'The things I said—last week. I'm sorry. I know they're not true.'

There was silence, then Emma was surprised to feel his hand on her arm. He gave it a gentle squeeze. 'I don't blame you for saying them,' he said, his voice gruff. 'I deserved a great deal worse.'

Emma shook her head. 'No. You didn't deserve those sorts of things to be said.' She turned and looked up at him. 'I know about Mrs Ashleigh.'

He had been looking at her, his fine eyes clear and soft. Now he coloured and quickly looked away. He made an inarticulate sound. Emma judged it to be a sound of dismissal. It was as Virginia had said. He hadn't wanted her to know about his kind deed.

'And—the Pettits. I know you do care.'

He didn't look up. Staring straight ahead, he asked softly, 'Did I make you think I didn't?'

Emma swallowed. 'Perhaps—I chose to interpret you that way.'

Patrick said nothing for a moment. She felt his hand tighten again on her arm. 'I wasn't at my best that day,' he said in a low voice, full of wry self-mockery.

'I'm sorry,' said Emma, and his grip became almost painful.

'Don't,' he said in a constricted voice. 'I'm sorry, too. I can't tell you how sorry I am that things have worked out this way. I would give almost anything for it to be different. It seems there's nothing I can do.'

Yes! Emma cried inwardly. Love me and leave Prudence. She knew it was something she could never say. Aloud she simply told him, 'I understand.'

He sat with her a little longer in silence, his strong brown hand still clasped around her wrist as though he had forgotten it was there. Emma couldn't forget it. It filled her with a kind of agony to be touched by him. She was acutely aware of every beloved feature of the strong dark man sitting tensely at her side. Then, to her relief, he was called away, and Emma continued there, reflecting. The sooner he left here the better. Just a few moments of gentleness from him was enough to rekindle every tender feeling and banish the memory of his harshness to the back of her mind. She thought about the day when he would leave, and was filled with such pain that she suddenly wondered if half a loaf might be better than no bread after all. But when she thought of what that would mean—the secrecy and the lying, and the knowing that he belonged to someone else—she knew it would only destroy her.

'Looks like the southerly change is on its way,' Marje said. 'You'll be lucky to get to the bus before it rains, Emma.'

Emma looked out of the window of the waiting-room. 'It can't come soon enough for me. It's been like midsummer today.' Sure enough the black clouds that presaged the southerly were massing overhead. It was Sydney's saving grace, this wind that often came up in the afternoon to relieve the sweltering summer heat. It usually brought rain, and that kept the gardens alive through the hot season. Patrick came out and looked over her shoulder.

'You're going to get wet.' His deep voice startled her. 'You'd better let me drive you home.'

'No, it's all right, thanks,' she said. 'It'll be fifteen minutes yet.' She threw him a quick smile over her shoulder to show she was grateful for the offer and ducked out of the door.

The following day was just as hot. Midsummer had come early. They opened all the windows in the clinic and had the fan on full speed. It was still more pleasant at lunchtime to go and eat outside in the shade of the trees. There was a light nor'-easter there. Helen joined her for a while, then after she had gone to do some shopping Patrick came outside again. She made room for him, then stuck her feet back up on the crate she was using as a stool. She tried to relax, to continue unconcernedly eating her sandwiches, but she was conscious of the same tension as yesterday at his presence. Why was he seeking her company in this way? He stretched his long legs out before him and folded his arms across his chest.

'I'll miss the sun,' he said, and Emma felt a sharp stab of pain at the mention of his going away. As she had done so many times, she absently stroked the scar on her leg. It was too hot for tights now, and Emma hadn't worn them today. She finished her sandwiches and screwed up the paper bag, turning to toss it into the bin at the back door. When she turned back she saw Patrick looking at the scar. He put out his hand as though to touch it, then seemed to think better of it. 'What's that?' he asked softly. 'You didn't have that before.'

Emma's heart sped as all at once the strongest desire arose in her to tell him. If she told him, perhaps he would stop being angry with her. One of the feelings at least that plagued him might be gone. It could heal the hurt he'd felt and make him forgive her.

'I had a lump removed,' she said with some difficulty. 'A cyst.'

What would be the outcome if she told him the rest? Would it make him happier? Suddenly Emma realised that it was not entirely Patrick's happiness that impelled her to tell him. It was her own. Against all reason, hope still lived in her—hope that if she told him he would love her again, and would break it off with Prudence.

'What sort of cyst?' he asked her, and she told him. He frowned. 'That must have been worrying at first.'

He was so close to the truth. Should she tell him? Emma tried desperately to think clearly. 'Yes,' she answered. 'It was for a day or two. Till the pathology result came through.'

'Poor Emma,' he said softly. 'When was this?'

Emma stood poised on a knife-edge. How would it be? What would he say?

'Emma, John Morrison's on the phone for you.' Marje's voice made her jump.

Emma jerked around. 'Oh—yes. OK, Marje. I'll be there in a second.' She glanced at Patrick. His face had become immobile. She opened her mouth but could say nothing. She went to answer the phone.

Sister Treloar worked through the long warm afternoon automatically doing the job she had come to know so well. As she worked she found time to wonder. Why hadn't she told him? It hadn't just been John's call that had prevented her from taking the plunge. It was some sort of cowardice. Emma finally came to the conclusion that she was afraid to hear what he would say. For she realised the most likely thing was that it wouldn't make any difference at all. If there was any chance that Patrick could love her again in the way he had before, she would know about it by now. Not for one moment had he led her to believe that he would give up Prudence for her. He had merely let her know that he had feelings for them both. But those he had for her would not be allowed to break up his relationship. And that she couldn't bear to hear him say. She was glad she hadn't told him. In three weeks he would be gone, and it would no longer matter what he thought about her and what had happened in the past.

CHAPTER THIRTEEN

THE storm had already broken that day by the time
Emma was ready to leave. It was as dark as twilight
outside though it was only five-thirty, and the rain was
coming down in sheets and swirling away down the
gutters.

'I knew there was something I meant to bring to
work today,' she said.

'What's that, love?' asked Marje.

'An umbrella,' Emma told her drily.

'Oh, lord. You're going to be drowned. I'd better
walk you to your stop with mine.'

Patrick had just placed his files on the receptionists'
desk. 'It's all right, Marje. I can run Emma home.
You, too, if you like.'

'Bless your heart, Dr Patrick,' she said. 'I don't need
a lift. Frank's coming to pick me up. But you take
Emma, else she'll be soaked to the skin.'

One more look outside convinced Emma that it
would be foolish, and exceedingly wet, to argue.
'Thanks,' she said simply.

As it was, the dash to the car wet them both quite
a bit. They piled into it, gasping and dripping water,
and slammed the doors. A number of traffic jams and
minor accidents made their progress slow, and the rain
was beginning to slacken when they pulled up outside
Emma's place.

Patrick peered through the windscreen and suddenly
grinned. 'Is that your cat?' he asked.

Emma looked out and saw a bedraggled creature

pressed against the front door. She couldn't help giggling. 'Yes,' she said. 'But he's not looking his best.'

Patrick gave a short laugh.

'Thank you,' Emma said, striving for calm. 'It was kind of you to drive me.' She put her hand on the door-handle to get out and heard Patrick say her name. She turned to him.

'May I—may I come in?' he asked.

Emma's pulse speeded up. A knot gathered in the pit of her stomach. Why? she thought. But she said nothing, trying to think of a polite way to say no.

'This may sound stupid,' he told her, answering her unspoken question, 'but—soon I'll be thousands of miles away.' He turned to look at her. 'I want to see where you live.'

'Why?' she said softly.

'I don't know,' he said. 'Just—so I can picture you.'

Emma felt a sudden rush of overwhelming sadness. He did care about her in some way. And she understood what he meant. That had been one of the hardest things after he had left—not even to be able to imagine where he was. She nodded, a lump in her throat, and he slid out of the car.

Tiger stalked into the house before her in dudgeon, managing to convey somehow that he held her personally responsible for the rain. Emma led the way to the kitchen, and Patrick followed slowly, looking around. Tossing her bag on to the bench, Emma sought a towel, and gave herself a brief wipe with it before handing it to Patrick.

'He looks like he needs it more than me,' Patrick remarked of the cat. Tiger assented by shaking himself disgustedly. He said he hated to be wet.

'Actually, I lied to you. I'm afraid he doesn't look much better dry,' Emma said.

Patrick laughed, that deep, resonant laugh. There was a moment's silence, when Emma couldn't think what to do next. 'Would you like a cup of tea?' she asked finally, and when he accepted thought, Thank God for tea. Whatever would we do without it?

They sat with their tea in the sitting-room, and Emma watched Patrick look around him. It was a cheerful room that reflected her personality. There were plenty of books, some pot-plants, a colourful rug and bright modern prints on the walls. Some of them he might have remembered from before. He sank back in Emma's favourite armchair, and fell silent. Emma was silent, too, watching him as he seemed to study a print on the wall. She knew that she would always remember Patrick Cavanagh sitting there like that.

He dropped his eyes to her suddenly and caught her own upon him. He gave a small sad smile. 'Why did you move from the other place?' he asked.

Emma decided to be honest. 'Memories,' she said.

He looked at her for a long moment. 'Of us?'

She nodded, and there was another pause.

Then he said slowly, 'Were they so painful?'

Emma nodded again, and spoke, her voice a whisper. 'I didn't mean to do what I did to you.'

Patrick looked down at his feet. 'I don't suppose you did. In any case, it doesn't matter. It's past.'

It was true. It was past, and it didn't matter to him any more—only to Emma. And she couldn't tell him just how much it mattered to her. There wasn't any point. She wished suddenly that he would go, but he only got up to wander restlessly about the room. Finally he stopped in front of a print. 'I remember this,' he said, his back towards her. Then slowly he turned and said in a low voice, 'I wonder why I can't stop wanting you when I know it's impossible?'

Emma sat still, only her heart thudding in her chest. He came towards her and knelt beside her chair. 'It's impossible,' he repeated. 'And I can't change that.'

Why? Emma wanted to cry. Why can't you stop wanting *her*? She said nothing, but the tears welled up in her eyes.

Patrick took her hands in his suddenly and raised them to his lips. 'Don't! Don't, Emma!' he said in an agonised tone. 'I didn't come here to make you cry! I'm sorry!'

But the tears wouldn't stop. He watched them a moment, his face full of pain, then pulled her into his arms. 'Don't, Emma. Don't cry,' he said hoarsely. 'It doesn't matter.'

What did he mean it didn't matter? It might not matter to him. Once back in England, away from her, with someone he loved better than her, he'd forget all about this midsummer madness, this return to the past. Emma felt she would live in the past all her days.

She became aware of his hands stroking her back. She felt him kiss her hair. They were silent. Then, 'Emma, are you sure?' he cried in a voice that seemed torn from him. He took her face between his hands and turned it up to him, saying in an urgent tone, 'Look at me. Look at me, please!'

Emma raised her face to him, the tears spilling out and running over her cheeks. He looked deep into her eyes. His voice was a hoarse whisper. 'Whenever I touch you, whenever I kiss you, I can't accept that I can't have you. Some part of you wants me like you did before—I'm willing to swear it.' He bent forward and quickly brushed her lips with his own. Then he sat back again, gazing into her eyes. 'Those eyes!' he said. 'Those sweet, grave, laughing grey eyes that say so much. How am I to respond to what they tell me, Emma? Do you know what they say now?'

She gave a sob and shook her head, still held between his hands. 'They say, Kiss me again, Patrick,' he whispered. His clear hazel eyes burned into her misty grey ones. 'How can I not obey, Emma, when it's what I want so much to do?'

Emma sobbed again and more tears fell. He kissed her wet cheeks and her eyes, then slowly brought his lips to hers again in a kiss whose tenderness wrung her heart. He moved his lips an inch back from hers and asked, 'Does it matter as much as this, Emma? That other person?' She stared into the eyes that she loved so much. 'Let me make love to you,' he whispered. 'Let me make you forget there's anyone else in the world.' The man's arms went round her again, and his lips once more fastened themselves to hers. But it was only for a moment. For Emma couldn't kiss him any longer. She was crying now in good earnest.

He watched her, his face full of concern. Emma swallowed and found her tongue. 'H-how can you ask me? Why? What is it we're to have? A night stolen from somebody else, so we can wake up in the morning a little more bitter and grieved than when we went to bed?' She took a painful breath. 'Is that what you want, Patrick?'

He dropped his eyes. 'No,' he said in a low, hollow voice. 'Not if that's how it would be.'

'That's how it would be!' she cried passionately. 'Maybe you can forget there's someone else, but I can't!'

Patrick moved back slowly. 'I see,' he said so softly that she barely heard him. He rose to his feet and walked to the window, looking out on the last of the rain.

'Why does it matter so much to you?' she cried in an anguished tone.

Patrick turned to face her, reading her pain in her features. 'It doesn't,' he said suddenly. His next words echoed her thoughts from before. 'It's a piece of madness. It's only a memory. I'd better go.'

He'd been gone a long time before Emma was able to stop her tears.

Three weeks wore inexorably by, each day marked by Emma's growing anguish. She thought of taking holidays and going away somewhere so she didn't have to live through this agonising time. But she couldn't bring herself to do it. Each minute with Patrick was painful, but each was also precious. Somehow, in the imminence of his departure, any anger she had felt for him had gone. He couldn't be blamed for caring for someone else more than her. He couldn't be blamed for being angry with her. If blame were to be handed out it could only be for wanting to have Emma as well, for offering her the small change of his life. And Emma didn't feel like blaming any more.

'Well, he's really going,' said Helen one morning tea time. 'I just heard him make his airline reservation.'

'What a shame,' said Anne. 'I hope the next doctor'll be as good.'

'I wonder what the "personal reasons" are?' said Helen curiously.

'Might have family troubles at home,' suggested Anne.

'Maybe his spouse doesn't like it here,' put in Fiona. 'We haven't seen anything of her, have we? You'd think she would have come along to see where he worked and who he worked with.'

Helen shook her head. 'I think it's really sad when

all the patients like him so much. They're really upset he's going. What did he come for if he was only going to stay a few months?'

Emma for some reason felt impelled to defend him. 'I think he meant to stay,' she said quietly. 'Sometimes things just don't work out.'

Anne nodded, and Helen gave a sigh. Marje Gilbert, on the other hand, made a noise that sounded like 'Humph' and continued solidly and silently chomping her way through her fruit cake. Emma avoided her eye. She had more than once suspected that Marje, of all the people here, had the best idea of what had been going on. Helen and Anne had accepted with little surprise Emma's change from Patrick to Fiona's list. Disagreements arose sometimes in this sort of situation where people worked so closely on so many sensitive matters. Emma thought Fiona had been suspicious at first, but she seemed not to have thought any more about it. It was Marje who had looked at her from out of shrewd, frankly sceptical eyes when she had explained the change.

Two weeks from Dr Cavanagh's departure date, his replacement was brought to the centre by Evan Thomas, and there was a general sigh of relief. No one more different from Patrick could be found, but there was a common feeling that he would be all right. He was a friendly, cheerful man, disgustingly fat for a doctor, Helen said. Emma thought he looked more like an opera singer than a doctor, though perhaps that was partly because of his powerful voice and his ringing laugh. His name was Jim Barnard and Emma thought he would probably be a lot of fun and a favourite with the patients in no time flat.

If Patrick had any sad feelings at showing his successor round, he kept them to himself. It was he who introduced Emma to the new doctor.

'Just do whatever this one tells you, Jim,' he said, 'and you can't go wrong. There's not much she doesn't know.'

Jim Barnard's laugh rang out. 'I'm used to doing what I'm told,' he said with a twinkle. 'I've got four daughters.'

Emma laughed. Yes, she was going to like this man. In the next moment she was swamped with ineffable sadness. It was the thought of life going on without Patrick, and with someone else in his place. For a second her eyes met with Patrick's and she saw her own feelings reflected there. Any amusement had fled and there was a look of desolation in his face to take its place. He gave her a small painful smile, and as Jim looked around him, exclaiming at how well-equipped they were, Patrick put an arm round her shoulder and just for a moment hugged her to his side.

Emma had to flee. She took refuge in the bathroom, and cried there, as she had done several times before.

The last week came, with weather so hot that Emma could have cheerfully packed up and emigrated to Britain herself. There was a general envy of Patrick who would soon be somewhere cold.

'Oh! Dr Patrick—can I stow away in your suitcase?' Helen asked, collapsing into a chair. 'Emma, why don't you do something? Make your John get us some air-conditioning.'

Emma would have protested that he wasn't her John, but the others had enthusiastically taken up the idea.

'Yeah! Do it, Emma. You know you only have to ask. Why are we sweltering?'

The days followed one another, hot and leaden. Emma dragged herself through them, coming home at night to cry. Virginia was there almost every evening just to be with her. She made Emma eat something, sat with her and fed the cat.

'It'll be better when he's gone, Em,' she said gently.

Emma nodded dully, the tears once more coursing down her face. Even Tiger seemed to sense she was unhappy. He took the unprecedented step of jumping up on her and sitting on her lap, seriously studying her face. What's the matter with you? he asked sternly. Pull yourself together.

Emma wanted nothing more than to pull herself together. But it seemed to be beyond her power. Every time she saw Patrick a new wave of grief racked her. When he wasn't there, it was a gnawing ache. She caught herself looking at him whenever she could as if to memorise everything about him. She secretly studied the strong, tanned face with its sensual curving mouth and fine light eyes. She looked at the shape of his ears, the way his brown hair grew, the sprinkling of grey at the side. Her eyes traced the lines of him— the strong neck, the broad shoulders, the powerful bulge of his thighs. His arms and hands held her gaze. She noted the shape of the long fingers, the size of his hands. She watched the muscular forearm as he stirred his tea, his shirt-cuffs turned up in the heat.

If he was aware of her scrutiny, he gave no sign. Only sometimes Emma thought he was doing the same thing with her. Once she had looked round in the staffroom and he had seemed to be studying her neck, or perhaps her ear. He had put out his hand then, and gently stroked her nape where the short hair that couldn't be put in her roll lay in a soft curl.

Emma had ached with love and sorrow. She had wanted to throw herself into his arms. She'd wanted to cling there, to cry, to beg him, Don't go. I'll do anything. Don't go. For a dizzy moment she'd thought of it. But she'd known she would only be condemning herself to a continuation of pain. She'd stood still, looking down at her knotted hands. And he had seemed to master himself. He had taken his hand away, and left her alone.

'I haven't lost a doctor, I've gained a cat,' Helen said on the second last day. 'I don't know how I've let myself be talked into this.'

'Are you taking Dr Patrick's cat?' asked Anne.

'He couldn't find anyone else silly enough,' Helen told her.

His last day at work arrived, and Emma wondered how the day could dawn like any other, and the sun still shine. She got through it somehow, silent and suffering. Patrick had declined a farewell party and Emma was glad. She couldn't have gone. One by one at the end of the day they said their goodbyes to him. Emma stayed till last, scrubbing out the treatment-room. She heard his footsteps approach finally and steeled herself as much as she could for the last ordeal.

He stood in the doorway of the room, and Emma faced him, leaning against the bench on the other side. She knew she couldn't bear to drag this out.

'Goodbye,' was all she said.

He looked at her for a long moment, his face pale and still. He opened his mouth to speak and it came out in a whisper. 'Goodbye.'

That was all there was. There was nothing more to say.

CHAPTER FOURTEEN

SOMEHOW Emma endured the weekend. Virginia came to see her on Saturday morning and again on Sunday afternoon. She dragged Emma out for a walk.

'When does his flight go?' Ginny asked.

'Monday. Tomorrow,' said Emma. 'Twelve noon.'

'Are you sure you should go to work tomorrow, Em?'

Emma nodded her head. 'It'll keep me busy. It'll force me to think of something else.'

'You might not feel too good around that time.'

'I think I'll feel better, Ginny. At least I won't have this terrible feeling that I want to call him.'

Ginny nodded, and gave her a hug as they walked. Emma looked at her friend through watery eyes. 'Has anyone ever told you you're the best friend in the world?' she asked.

Ginny hugged her again.

Emma slept little, and when she did it was made hideous by nightmares. She dreamed all kinds of things, but they all centred on Patrick Cavanagh. She was searching for him in a huge milling crowd. She saw him, but couldn't reach him. And then he disappeared again. She heard him calling her. He was standing at the foot of her bed. But when she awoke he wasn't there.

She was awake for good at five o'clock. It was hot and close already. It was going to be a hellish day. She left for work early, unable to think of anything else to do. It was impossible not to look for his car

176

when she got to the clinic, but of course it wasn't there. Emma opened the centre with her key and turned on the fan in the waiting-room that good, kind John had got them. Why couldn't she love John? she asked herself. There was no answer. She just didn't. Emma tidied the consulting-rooms, just to fill up time. One by one the others arrived and the clinic got under way.

All through the morning Emma was acutely aware of the time. Nine-thirty. They might be packing the last of their things. Ten-fifteen. Time to think of heading to the airport. Ten forty-five. They would probably be there. Time for morning tea came, and Emma, unable to bear company, poured a cup of tea she didn't want and went outside. It was eleven o'clock. One hour and Patrick Cavanagh might as well be on another planet. Emma gave a grim laugh. He might as well be on another planet now.

'I think I'll join you,' came Helen's voice from behind her. 'It's fractionally cooler out here. Have you spoken to John about the air-conditioning?'

Emma wanted to scream at her to go away. She couldn't do it. She only shook her head.

'I think I'll ring him and tell him to come and have a look at his sweetheart, wilting in the heat. That ought to do it. You look worse than I feel, Emma.'

'I'm all right,' Emma muttered.

Helen sat down and sighed. 'God, Patrick's so lucky. I wish I were going.'

Emma gritted her teeth.

Helen chatted on. 'I really fell for it with that cat. Prudence! He should have called her Reckless. Last night she knocked all the pots off the windowsill and this morning she climbed on the—Emma, are you all right?'

Emma wasn't listening. The entire world had tilted

beneath her feet. She sat motionless, blind and deaf to all around her, as her brain spun like a planet off its orbit. She couldn't say a word. She couldn't even think. She could only stare at Helen, her mouth open, her face the colour of a corpse.

'Emma, are you all right? Do you want to lie down? Is it the heat?'

Helen's voice permeated the maelstrom of her mind. She heard the worry. 'Yes. The heat,' she said faintly, and let Helen lay her down on the seat.

'Shall I get a wet towel?' Helen asked, but Emma managed to shake her head.

'No. I'm all right now.' Slowly her mind began to function. Had she imagined what Helen had said? 'Helen, what were you saying? What did Patrick call his cat?'

'Prudence,' Helen said. 'Stupid name. I suppose it was—what do you call it?—irony.'

Emma had stopped listening again. In direct contrast to a moment ago when it seemed that her brain was permanently paralysed, it now began to work with the speed of an express train.

Was it possible? Could it be? It was totally fantastic. Her mind went into rapid rewind and located the memory of that very first day. She heard their conversation again through the treatment-room door, or rather Patrick's part of it. 'Prudence. My companion.'

Why? It was crazy! But it wasn't. She heard the conversation again and quickly understood. She heard Fiona's voice—the unwelcome interest. His hesitation, embarrassment, the master-stroke he'd pulled to fend her off. He hadn't lied. He'd just forgotten to mention that his companion was a cat.

Emma began to laugh hysterically. She covered her mouth with her hand, but found she couldn't stop.

'Emma, I'm going to get one of the doctors,' Helen said. 'You're not well.'

'No!' Emma gasped. 'I'm all right!' But Helen had gone. Emma's mind resumed its frantic pace.

She had assumed the same as Fiona—that he was living with someone, already attached. But he must be! Or what did all those conversations mean? Emma's brain did another fast rewind, and played them all again. Never, not once, had they mentioned a name. Never had he come out and said, I'm with someone else. Unable to bring themselves to speak of it openly, all their references had been oblique. They could just as easily have been talking of someone in Emma's life.

'Let me make you forget there's anyone else in the world.' Words and phrases came back to her like meteors whirling out of space. Scenes, expressions, feelings—things only half understood at the time—raced through her mind till the chaos seemed to crystallise into one terrible and wonderful idea. He thought she loved John and, for all her evident faithlessness, wouldn't give him up. He probably thought she had been involved with John two years ago. There was no one in his life. She had done it to him again.

When Helen returned with Dr Fiona, they found Emma Treloar sitting bolt upright, staring ahead as though she had had a vision of hell.

'Emma, are you——?' Fiona began, but got no further, for Emma seemed to come to life.

She looked at Fiona with wild wide eyes. 'What time is it?' she asked hoarsely.

Fiona didn't answer straight away. She looked at Emma with concern and started to speak again.

'What time is it?' Emma cried in a desperate voice, and grabbed the doctor's arm to look at her watch. It was quarter-past eleven. Emma swore volubly. Then without another word she got up and hurled herself towards the door.

Jim Barnard, on his first day in his new job, was surprised to see Sister Treloar erupt through the back door of the clinic as though she were pursued by all the devils in hell. He was even more surprised to see her grab her bag and fling at the receptionist, 'Marje! I'm going!' before she flew down the hall. The calm way in which Marjorie Gilbert received it made him wonder if this was a regular occurrence. 'Yes, love,' was all Marje said.

There were taxis on the rank. Several passers-by turned to stare at the sight of a girl in nurse's uniform pelting down the footpath in a full sprint.

'Get me to Sydney Airport in fifteen minutes and I'll give you fifty dollars!' she flung at the driver. He stared at her a second. 'Well?' she cried, and tore the note from her purse.

He looked at it. 'You're on,' he said, and pulled out from the curve with a screech of tyres.

'And a cat,' added Emma under her breath. 'A cat called Prudence.'

It was certainly the most death-defying drive that Emma had ever experienced. But she knew no fear as the cabbie, his blood up and his pride on the line, broke every traffic rule in the handbook. They shot the orange light with another squeal of tyres as they turned into Cleveland Street, but Emma didn't flinch. When the driver hesitated for a moment at the corner of Cleveland and Dowling, Emma yelled, 'Go for it!' and he did, making a hair-raising turn across the oncoming traffic.

'Good God!' she heard him mutter.

Emma looked at the cabbie's watch. Her own was

on the sink at the clinic. Eleven twenty-five. 'Is your watch right?' she demanded.

'Yeah,' he nodded, concentrating on weaving in and out of the traffic. 'I set it by the radio.'

Eleven twenty-five. He probably would have boarded. She would need all the time she could save to somehow get him off the flight.

'There's nothing in the kerb lane,' Emma said, and the cabbie pulled into it.

'There's a parked car!' he exclaimed.

'It's a long way away,' said Emma. 'Put your foot down!' The cabbie did it. As they pulled back into the centre lane with feet to spare, he said a rude word.

In and out of the traffic they wove, treating orange lights like green and occasionally according the same treatment to a red one. Emma alternately thanked God for the celebrated sense of adventure of Sydney cabmen and cursed as they were forced to halt at a light, the minutes ticking away with agonising rapidity. 'Oh, God! Come on, come on!' she groaned at the traffic in front, beating her fist on the dashboard.

It took them thirteen minutes. It must have been some sort of record. In front of the international terminal, Emma thrust the fare and the fifty at the cabbie, said, 'You're a prince!' and scrambled out of the cab. She was running as soon as her feet hit the pavement.

Up till now she'd been calm except for her anguish at the passing of time, but as she swept into the thronging crowds of Sydney Airport, she knew a moment of blind panic. Eleven thirty-three, the clock overhead said, and even as she watched it flipped over to thirty-four. Her scalp prickled. Her heart thudded more violently than it had done before. She began to feel short of breath. Don't fall apart now! she cried inwardly, and made an effort to control herself. She turned and took

off at a run again towards the flight departures board.
Thank God she knew his flight. Helen had said he was
flying Qantas.

Emma weaved her way in and out of the moving
sea of travellers, narrowly avoiding inflicting grievous
bodily harm on a number of them. A man stood in
front of her, blocking her view of the departures board.
She grabbed him by the arm and thrust him aside. He
stared at her in amazement. The code for the flight to
London had a flashing boarding sign beside it. Gate
16. Emma looked around wildly, caught sight of the
sign and took to her heels again. Her heart pounded
and sweat trickled down her back as she ran up the
escalator. The clock overhead said eleven thirty-six,
tauntingly. 'Oh, please, get out of my way!' she said
desperately to the stationary person in front of her.

She ducked around a dawdling family at the top,
and resumed her headlong flight towards the last gate
at the end of the concourse. 'God, please God,' she
prayed. Passengers and well-wishers stopped and
stared as they caught sight of a young nurse running
full-tilt along the concourse as though her life
depended on it. Emma thought as she ran. What will
I do? Can I bribe them to take him a message? Can
I beg them? Tell them he's a dangerous lunatic escaped
from the hospital? Emma gave a sobbing laugh as she
ran. She knew she was the one who looked like a
lunatic. It would all take time. And that was something
she was fast running out of.

And then, as she reached the end of the concourse,
her heart leapt into her mouth. It seemed a major
miracle. She only saw him from behind, but she
instantly knew him. Three passengers were left to
board. And Patrick Cavanagh was one of them. Joy
burst inside her like an exploding star. She stood, sway-

ing and fighting for breath, and tried to call his name.
But she hadn't the breath left to say it. Horror-struck,
she watched the attendant return his pass as he stepped
through the doorway into Customs, where only other
passengers could follow. A cold sweat bathed her; her
heart turned over. But she wasn't finished yet. In des-
peration Emma acted.

She dropped her bag where she stood and vaulted
the barrier. A surprised ground attendant sprang
forward to block her path, but she took him by the
coat and hurled him aside bodily. She plunged ahead
through the doorway. She reached Patrick in a few
giant strides and grabbed him by the coat-tails. He
turned round, his eyebrow raised in the beginnings of
a question. Then he saw her. He stood stock-still, as
though in suspended animation.

Sweat ran down Emma's face. She trembled. She
was gasping. But she had just enough left for the barest
whisper. 'Patrick. Don't go. I love you!'

Seconds later, a number of nonplussed attendants
had gathered round the crumpled body of a girl in
nurse's uniform, lying inert on the floor of the Customs
hall. But the tall, dark passenger had taken charge,
and hoisted her into his arms.

'Hey—you have to board! This aircraft's leaving,'
said one of the attendants as he walked away.

The man turned at that, and said politely, 'Thank
you. I've changed my mind,' and kept walking.

When Emma came to, she was lying full-length on a
sofa. There was a wet towel on her forehead, and she
was looking up into Patrick's face. She realised her
head was in his lap.

'Where am I?' she asked shakily.

'In the Qantas business-class lounge,' he said. Then

all at once she was looking up at the loveliest sight in the world. For Patrick Cavanagh had smiled at her—a full, curving smile that invaded his eyes and made them shine like firelight.

'I love you, too,' he said simply.

Emma gazed up at him, and realised that it was more than the smile that made his eyes shine like that. It was joy, and love and tenderness. Slowly he bent his head and kissed her. It was the long, slow kiss she had dreamed of, in which their souls seemed to meet and intermingle.

Tears had sprung to Emma's eyes. 'I've been such an idiot!'

'I don't care,' he whispered. 'Just tell me you love me again.'

Emma twined her arms around his neck, and gave a little sob. 'I love you. I love you,' she told him. It was a long time before he let her speak again.

Then she looked mistily around her. 'Do you think we'll get into trouble for doing this in the business-class lounge?' she asked guiltily.

Patrick grinned. 'After your performance, I don't think anything will surprise them.'

Emma gave a little sobbing laugh. 'Oh, God,' she said. 'You've got no idea. I don't think I can tell you.'

'Don't tell me, then,' he said quickly, his arms tightening round her. 'It doesn't matter.'

'It does,' she cried. 'I have to tell you. Patrick—did you think I was—with John?'

He looked at her. 'Weren't you?' he asked slowly.

She shook her head. 'No. Never. No one.' She saw him frown, not understanding. Emma took a deep breath. 'There wasn't anyone this time, and there wasn't anyone last time. I lied to you then.'

Patrick Cavanagh gazed at her steadily, frowning a little. 'Why?' he whispered.

'So you would believe I didn't want to marry you.' Patrick Cavanagh waited, still uncomprehending. In a low voice, Emma told him, 'That thing on my leg. I found it the day before the holidays. Watts said he was sure it was an osteosarcoma. When I went for an open biopsy just before you left, I expected to wake up without my leg.'

Emma didn't need to say any more. She saw in his eyes the swift horror of full comprehension. Without a word Patrick picked her up in his arms and crushed her to his chest in an embrace that told of his feelings. When finally he released her a little later, his face was wet with tears.

'We'll talk of this,' he said with difficulty. 'But I can't now.' He gazed down at her for a long moment before he spoke again, in his eyes a fierce mixture of joy and relief and pain. 'Then—why this time?' he asked finally.

'That's the bit I *really* don't want to tell you,' she said, biting her lip.

'It can't be—as bad as that,' he said haltingly.

'It's even more stupid. I thought you were living with someone.' Emma swallowed. 'I eavesdropped.'

He shook his head. 'I don't understand you.'

'I heard you tell Fiona about your companion. Prudence. Only today—Helen said Prudence was a—a cat!'

There was a brief moment as it sank in. Then Patrick Cavanagh took a deep breath, threw back his head and roared with laughter. He laughed for a long, long time. When he'd finished, his face was wet again, this time for a different reason. He gasped, 'Truly, Emma—we were just good friends.'

And finally, as the utter absurdity of it all struck her, Emma started to laugh too. Patrick held her again and they shook with it, peal after peal.

'Oh, God, Emma.' He wiped his eyes, and sobered suddenly. He looked at her with sudden pain. His hoarse voice recalled what she now knew was their dual suffering. 'It wasn't very funny at the time, was it?'

Emma shook her head. She buried her face in his shoulder and hugged him hard. His strong arms tightened again. 'I'm surprised you still care,' he said in a low voice. 'I've behaved vilely. I loved you so much. When I first came, I tried not to feel anything. It was impossible. Then—I couldn't stand the thought of you with anyone else. Not—not John, especially. I couldn't understand it. He just wasn't right for you. I couldn't accept that I couldn't make you love me.'

'I always loved you. And it doesn't matter,' she whispered. 'I understand.'

'When I think of what I did, how I treated you. . .' He looked at her suddenly, a new thought dawning. 'And you believed I was—my God, what a fine fellow you must have thought me!'

Emma swallowed. 'I was a little cross with you,' she said in masterly understatement. 'I thought you wanted both of us.'

He looked at her with sad eyes. 'I could never offer you something like that,' he murmured.

'I know that now,' she said. 'But—I knew you had reason to be angry with me.'

He gathered her into his arms again. 'Yes, I was angry with you. You'd torn my heart out. But I never stopped loving you. And I had to come back. I just couldn't accept what had happened.'

'I tried to find you!' she cried. 'Lord, how I tried to find you!'

Patrick's strong arms gripped her tightly, his handsome face looking down at her. The light in the clear hazel eyes seemed to bathe her in warmth. 'Here I am,' he whispered. 'I'll never leave you.'

Some time later Emma Treloar sat up and straightened her uniform. She gave a sigh. 'I said some awful things to you. I behaved badly, too.'

Patrick looked down at her fondly. 'No, my Emma.' Then his eyes twinkled, and he added, 'Except perhaps in the departure lounge. I think the ground attendant you manhandled has a whiplash injury.'

Emma gave him her most impish grin. 'You should have seen the cabbie. *He* had a nervous breakdown.'

Some time later, a tall, good-looking man and a rather dishevelled nurse emerged from the Qantas lounge, the man with his arm about her. They walked slowly across the terminal, deep in discussion.

'I need a new job,' Patrick Cavanagh observed.

'I think we need three doctors at the clinic,' said Emma. 'We could easily convert the storage-room.'

'We'll think about it when we've returned from a long honeymoon,' said Patrick firmly.

'You know, Patrick, I don't think Helen really likes Prudence. I think we're going to be a two-cat family.'

He groaned.

Emma grinned up at him. 'Look on the bright side,' she said. 'It'll cheer Tiger right up.'

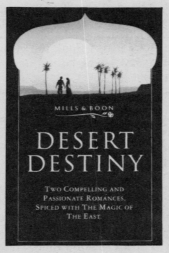
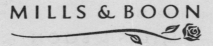

HEARTS OF FIRE

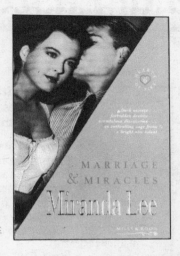

Gemma's marriage to Nathan is in tatters, but she is sure she can win him back if only she can teach him the difference between lust and love…

She knows she's asking for a miracle, but miracles can happen, can't they?

The answer is in Book 6…

MARRIAGE & MIRACLES
by Miranda Lee

The final novel in the compelling HEARTS OF FIRE saga.

Available from August 1994   Priced: £2.50

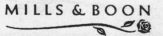

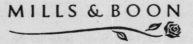

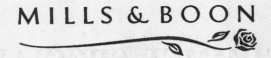

MILLS & BOON

LOVE ON CALL

The books for enjoyment this month are:

HEARTS OUT OF TIME Judith Ansell
THE DOCTOR'S DAUGHTER Margaret Barker
MIDNIGHT SUN Rebecca Lang
ONE CARING HEART Marion Lennox

♥   ♥   ♥   ♥   ♥

Treats in store!

Watch next month for the following absorbing stories:

ROLE PLAY Caroline Anderson
CONFLICTING LOYALTIES Lilian Darcy
ONGOING CARE Mary Hawkins
A DEDICATED VET Carol Wood

LOVE ON CALL
4 FREE BOOKS AND 2 FREE GIFTS
FROM MILLS & BOON

Capture all the drama and emotion of a hectic medical world when you accept 4 Love on Call romances PLUS a cuddly teddy bear and a mystery gift - absolutely FREE and without obligation. And, if you choose, go on to enjoy 4 exciting Love on Call romances every month for only £1.80 each! Be sure to return the coupon below today to: Mills & Boon Reader Service, FREEPOST, PO Box 236, Croydon, Surrey CR9 9EL.

✂ — — — — —┤ **NO STAMP REQUIRED** ├— — — — —

YES! Please rush me 4 FREE Love on Call books and 2 FREE gifts! Please also reserve me a Reader Service subscription, which means I can look forward to receiving 4 brand new Love on Call books for only £7.20 every month, postage and packing FREE. If I choose not to subscribe, I shall write to you within 10 days and still keep my FREE books and gifts. I may cancel or suspend my subscription at any time. I am over 18 years. Please write in BLOCK CAPITALS.

Ms/Mrs/Miss/Mr _____ **EP63D**

Address _____

_____

Postcode _____ Signature _____

MAILING PREFERENCE SERVICE